The Invisible Arrow

The Mason Braithwaite Paranormal
Mystery Series, book 6

Also in this series:

Praise for the series:

Every foray by Church's wonderful psychic detective Mason Braithwaite is a truly suspenseful page-turner in the most unusual crime series ever, and certainly one that no aficionado of crime fiction should miss.
—David Osborn, author of the best-selling Cold War thrillers *The French Decision* and *Love and Treason*

Mason is a hero like none who have come before him: a sensitive, queer P.I. whose only weapon is his intuition. This book turns the detective genre on its head and makes you think about the ninety percent of your brain you're not using.
—Teja Watson, author of *Attic.doc*

Another fast-paced ride through Los Angeles by Church, who continues to reinvent and reinvigorate Mason Braithwaite, keeping the Paranormal Mystery Series relevant and entertaining. Church's writing is vivid, the worlds he creates believable, and his characters have a breadth of humanity, strength, and vulnerability that makes the series a fun-filled, page-turning adventure.
—Jeremy Randolph, author of *The Mural*

Thanks to Christopher Church for giving us another exciting and well written adventure with one of my new heroes.
—Amos Lassen

The Invisible Arrow

The
Invisible
Arrow

Christopher Church

DAGMAR
MIURA
LOS ANGELES

Published by Dagmar Miura
Los Angeles
www.dagmarmiura.com

The Invisible Arrow

This is a work of fiction. Names, characters, businesses, places, events,
and incidents are either the products of the author's imagination or
used in a fictitious manner. Any resemblance to actual persons, living
or dead, or actual events is purely coincidental.

First published 2017

ISBN: 978-1-942267-32-4

ONE

M ason didn't really believe in ghosts, at least not in the Victorian sense, that they're dead people's essences floating around. Since he worked as a psychic, that often surprised people. But he was willing to be proven wrong, and if Yoshida was willing to part with some money to have him hunt one down, how could he argue? He was cycling over to Rugley Hall in Los Feliz, a community center where Yoshida kept an office, not far from Mason's neighborhood. He had worked with Yoshida, digging into some of Rugley Hall's secrets, and now Yoshida had summoned him for another job. The late-afternoon autumn sun was fading but it was still warm out, as it always was in Los Angeles late into the year, and he ran his hand-kerchief through his sweaty hair as he climbed off his bicycle in front of the redbrick building.

Locking his bike to a parking sign across the street, he admired the neoclassical facade, engraved at the top with the Masonic motto "Ordo ab Chao," order from chaos. He smiled at the memory of his time here. In a way it was what he was doing, helping people sort out their problems, creating order. He walked through the front door and past the little desk in the foyer for the security guard, who looked up long enough to give Mason the once-over.

Yoshida's office was down the corridor, gloriously unrenovated since the 1940s, behind the door with "103" painted on the frosted glass. Mason knocked gently before pushing it open to find Yoshida behind his desk. He looked up at Mason over his glasses, then rose, smiling broadly.

"The psychic investigator."

"You look good," Mason said, although Yoshida hadn't changed much since he'd seen him last, a cardigan draped over his rail-thin frame despite the warmth of the day. He was in his sixties, Mason guessed, and if anything he'd gone a little grayer over the past few months.

"You're flushed," Yoshida said, sitting down again and gesturing to one of the chairs in front of his desk. "Did you run here?"

Mason slipped off his backpack and dropped into the chair, setting the bag at his feet. "I cycled. The color is just the red-headed thing—not much pigment to hide the blood flow."

"I hope you wear sunscreen."

"So, how's business?" Mason asked.

"Good—we're having a fairly big event here this weekend, a regional Girl Scouts meeting. I'm not sure if it's just the leaders or the kids too, but they booked all the meeting rooms."

Mason grinned. "It sounds like you'll have your hands full either way." He'd meant Yoshida's paid work, in commercial real estate, not the volunteer work here at the community center. But the goings-on at Rugley Hall were almost certainly more interesting than the life of a landlord.

"On the phone you said something about a ghost infestation."

Yoshida's face clouded. "I thought of you because I know you can be discreet," he said. "And because the paranormal is your field. Have you looked into ghost activity before?"

"I don't have any experience with it, but I try to keep an open mind."

"Good," Yoshida said emphatically. "I think that's a reasonable starting point." He reclined in his chair.

"So is the ghost here? Did you see it yourself?" Mason pulled his yellow notepad and a pen out of his backpack, then turned to a blank page and wrote "Yoshida's ghost" across the top.

"Not me—my tenants keep complaining about it. It's in one of my commercial properties in North Chinatown."

It was disappointing that it wasn't here, Mason thought, writing his notes. He'd love to spend some more time poking around Rugley Hall.

"What did your tenants see?"

Yoshida sighed and started into the story. "It's a very old building, too rough to use as office space. I'm going to do a gut renovation, maybe next year, but for now I'm letting artists use it as studio spaces. They're there at all hours, and several of them have heard things—voices and machinery—and thought someone else was in the building. But when they look around, no one's there. One of the tenants did some reading and found out that an office worker, a woman, died in the building a long time ago, during the Depression. So his theory is that her ghost is haunting the place."

"Has he seen her?"

"You know what artists are like."

Mason looked up from his notes. "Not really."

Yoshida sought the right word. "They're emotional. He says he can visualize her, which sounds to me like he hasn't seen anything, just imagined it."

"What did he visualize?"

"A woman in a gray business suit, 1930s-style. She's gray too, he says, like a black-and-white photograph."

"That's interesting."

"Yeah, and annoying. If it was just the one guy, I'd tell him to up the dosage on his meds. But three of these artists moved in and then moved right back out again. They all said they heard voices through the walls in empty rooms. One young woman heard what she described as a circular saw. I'd like to find out what's going on, and without attracting attention."

"From the media?"

"And from ghost hunters. The last thing I need is tour buses pulling up at midnight and forty people traipsing through the place with the lights off. Imagine the liability."

"I get it," Mason said. "I'd love to look into it. What do you know about the office worker?"

"Nothing. The building is about a hundred years old. It was originally the headquarters of a security company—armed guards, safes, that kind of thing. There are rail yards all around there, and the security company worked with those businesses, guarding cargo and payroll delivery. It's right by the Cornfield, which used to be a rail yard too."

Mason nodded, scribbling the details on his pad. "I know the Cornfield. When should we go?"

"Oh, I don't think you'll need me there," Yoshida said. "The creative types said the ghost is usually active between midnight and three, so that's when you'll want to go."

"I can do that," Mason said, although he was leery about cycling that late at night, after a nighttime accident a while back.

"There's a lockbox outside with the front door key in it. It has a keypad, and you punch in a four-digit code to open it." He recited the number.

"That's so weird," Mason said, not bothering to write it down. "That's my roommate's birthday."

"Your boyfriend's?"

"No—Peggy, our housemate. At least I won't forget it."

Yoshida nodded. "It's called the Montclair Security Building, and the studio spaces are what we call open-plan."

"Meaning no walls?"

"There are walls, but all the internal doors are gone. I put in some lockers so they can store their materials, but mostly there's no private space."

"I can't wait. It sounds so bohemian."

Yoshida rubbed his chin. He looked tired. "It's grungy, Mason, and probably shouldn't have people in it. But I can't afford to gut it just yet."

Mason put his notepad away and stood up, slinging his bag onto his shoulder. "Does it matter what night I go?"

"Not at all," Yoshida said, rising and stepping around the desk. "Nobody will be there."

They shook hands and Mason left, closing the door behind him. A moment later Yoshida opened it again and called after him.

"Room 203," he said.

Mason spun around. "What?"

Yoshida glanced past Mason's shoulder and spoke just loud enough to be heard. "They say the noise seems to be coming from room 203."

"Got it," he said, making a mental note of the number and heading toward the entrance. He murmured good-bye to the security guard and went out to unlock his bike.

Twilight was just settling in, and it was already cooler, but the ride home was still a grind. The last quarter-mile to the house he shared with Ned and

Peggy was a steep incline, and even after doing it almost daily for years, he was still breathing hard when he reached the garage and parked his bike. But the climb was worth it, as the living room and the balcony had a nice view over their little neighborhood and the sun setting in the west.

As he walked in and put his bag down, Peggy came up the hall from her room, already changed out of her somber law-office garb into sweatpants and a T-shirt, her long brown hair tied loosely behind her head.

"How was work?" he asked.

"Boring," she said, and dismissed the matter with a wave of her hand. "Where were you?"

"I got a job. I'll tell you about it at dinner. You'll love it—ghost hunting."

"That does sound like fun."

"We are having dinner, aren't we? Where's Ned?" It was worrisome, because he was getting hungry. Both Ned and Peggy were enthusiastic about vegan cooking, which meant that apart from cleaning up and helping out once in a while with food prep, he ate well without having to do a whole lot of work.

"Gone to the market to get giant pasta shells. He's making cashew ricotta and stuffing it in the shells."

"That sounds like it'll be worth waiting for."

Mason went down the hall into the office he shared with Ned and got comfortable at his desk. He went through the notes he'd made with Yoshida, then stuffed them into a new file folder and wrote on the tab MONTCLAIR SECURITY BUILDING—GHOST. Before long he heard the garage door open and close again. Ned was home.

When he went out to the living room, Ned was already in the kitchen, tying on his apron. Mason sat on one of the barstools at the counter that separated the kitchen from the main room.

"Can I help?" Mason asked him.

Ned grinned. "You can tell me about your meeting. Do you want coffee?"

"Hit me," he said, and watched Ned set up the espresso maker. When it had filled the little pot, he poured a small amount into a demitasse cup for himself and dumped the bulk of it into a mug, sliding it across the counter to Mason.

As he watched Ned work, chopping spinach and mashing the soaked cashews into vegan cheese, Mason told him about Yoshida, the building by the Cornfield, and what the tenants had heard. Even in the kitchen Ned looked suave, his blue dress shirt nicely pressed under his apron, his dark hair natty no matter what he did. When they first met he'd thought Ned was so effortlessly put together because he was Latino, but over the last few years he'd gotten to know Ned's brothers, and they didn't have anything similar going on. It was all Ned.

Eventually the meal was ready, and Mason helped set everything on the dining table. Ned propped open the French doors to the balcony to let out the heat from the kitchen, and Mason called Peggy.

"Look at this feast," she said, sitting down with them. She asked Ned about the cashew ricotta technique, then turned to Mason. "So what's this about ghost hunting?"

He told her about the ghost and what the tenants had heard. "Yoshida said an office worker died there way back when, and one of the artists thinks he can visualize her."

"Was it a suicide?" she asked.

"No idea—why do you ask?" Mason said through a mouthful of pasta, and to Ned, "This is so good."

"She probably got bored to death working in an office. It sucks the life right out of you."

"It was during the Depression, so she was probably happy just to have a job," Mason said. "I don't know what to think about the whole ghost thing. It doesn't make sense to me that the essence of a dead person would just hang around an office building."

"That's surprising, coming from the guy who makes his living as a psychic," Ned said, cutting into a stuffed shell.

"Why is that surprising?" Mason asked, feeling his face heating up. "I'm not allowed to disbelieve the mainstream explanation?"

"Usually you believe anything—information encoded in jewelry, time-traveling desert rats."

Mason sighed. Ned was a committed nontheist, rejecting anything without scientific evidence to back it up. "I'm not sure what I believe about ghosts."

"Why is it about your beliefs?" Peggy asked, waving her fork. "It could be scientific. Maybe science just isn't capable of seeing ghosts yet."

Mason shook his head. "It's just too simple.

When people die, they're gone."

Ned sat back in his chair, looking at them. "Who are you, and what have you done with my psychic boyfriend?"

Mason ignored him and spoke to Peggy. "I don't mean they're gone forever. That individual personality is gone, but of course something still exists—other incarnations in other times, stuff like that."

"That sounds more like the man I know," Ned said, picking up his fork again.

"So if ghosts aren't dead people, what are they?" Peggy asked.

"Don't look at me," Mason said. "Ned's the one with all the answers."

Ned scowled. "I never said that. But I can tell you exactly what ghosts are. Machinery sometimes generates low-frequency sound waves that you can't hear consciously, but your brain still perceives it. It creeps people out and makes them think there's a malicious presence around."

"Seriously?" Peggy asked. "What kind of machinery?"

"Furnaces, air conditioners, even the pipes and ducts. Old buildings are more often 'haunted' because they have old machinery that's more prone to that kind of vibration."

"That seems like too simple an explanation," Mason said, pushing away his empty plate. "I'm going to ask Peggy's boyfriend what he thinks."

"How is Matt, by the way?" Ned asked.

"Things are great," Peggy said. "He's coming to

see me as Peggy Pregnant for the first time tomorrow night." Her true passion was music, and she performed at small venues around town as Peggy Pregnant, dressed in 1960s garb with a huge fake baby belly, singing folky tunes and playing an acoustic guitar.

"How is it possible you haven't performed for him yet?" Ned asked, incredulous. "You've been going out for months."

"I've played for him before, lots of times. I've just never let him come to a Peggy Pregnant gig."

"Why not?" Mason asked.

"He's a guy. I figured the pregnant persona would freak him out."

"But you're not really pregnant," Mason said.

"I know that," she said, irritated. "But Peggy Pregnant is. I guess it's about intimacy, showing him that part of me."

Mason didn't really understand, but he let it go. They sat in silence for a while as Ned and Peggy finished eating.

"When are you going to the haunted building?" Ned said finally.

"Not tonight—I want to do some research first. Maybe tomorrow. I have to go after midnight."

"Of course," he said. "It has to be dark and atmospheric."

Mason shook his head. "Such a skeptic."

"If you sense a ghost, look for pipes and machinery," Ned said. "Cut the power to the machine, and bye-bye ghost."

11

"Can I tag along?" Peggy asked. "It sounds like an adventure."

"Sure," Mason said. She wasn't a skeptic, like Ned, so she wouldn't be a killjoy. She accepted his psychic experiences and took him at his word.

Mason helped clean up and then sprawled on the sofa with Ned as he read a novel. Mason looked around online for good ghost phenomena sites. There was a lot of fluff and marketing, and there was a broad assumption among the many commentators that ghosts were real, not just a misinterpretation of more pedestrian events like creaking wooden stairs or mice in the attic. Weightier sources provided a range of explanations as to why dead people would hang around—a grudge against a living person, an untimely or unjust death—but they all fell into the category of unfinished business.

He didn't feel like he was learning much, so after Ned went into the bedroom, he closed his computer and tried to get some insight using his psychic senses. He spent a few minutes clearing his mind, pushing away the random thoughts that intruded, until he was calm and receptive. He imagined his senses expanding beyond his head, connecting with the world, open to whatever relevant information might appear. Yoshida came to mind, but that wasn't inspiration, just a memory, and he brushed it aside. He saw a fox, cute and red, peering at him and then darting away, its bushy tail gone as quickly as it had come. That didn't seem relevant, so he formulated a question and focused on it: *What's going on at Yoshida's building?*

No valid answers came to him, and eventually he gave up. It wasn't discouraging, because it had been a long shot anyway. He knew he had to gather more information in the real world before he could expect valid insights.

Later he followed Ned to bed. When Mason turned to kiss him good night, Ned was watching him with a gentle smile.

"What's so funny?"

He reached up and ran his fingers through Mason's hair. "I love that you don't believe that ghosts are ghosts. I need to remember not to make assumptions about how your mind works."

Mason closed his eyes and enjoyed Ned's fingers on his scalp. "My mind is like high-speed precision engineering, baby."

"I was thinking more like one of those whirlwinds you see in Central Valley. But it's a similar visual."

He chuckled and rolled over, letting Ned wrap his arm around him as they settled into sleep.

One of the techniques he used to get information from beyond his regular senses was lucid dreaming. Drifting into the hypnagogic state, he gave himself the suggestion to come to awareness inside the dream, take action, and hopefully get some ideas about Yoshida's ghost. Eventually he found himself in a bleak yard with gray concrete walls, surrounded by men milling around, wearing old-timey black-and-white prison stripes. He looked down at his sleeves and saw he was wearing them too. Another man caught his eye. "This is not a good place," he said gravely.

Mason was aware enough to know he was dreaming, and had no intention of lingering in such oppressive surroundings. He turned away, willing the scene to evaporate, willing himself awake. He clicked on the bedside light and scrabbled in the nightstand drawer for his pad and a pen. "In a prison yard," he wrote. "Black and white and gray." But there was something more, an insight just beyond his consciousness. His mind ached as he struggled to reach it, but eventually it came, and he wrote another line. "Gray, like the ghost in Yoshida's building."

TWO

esides Ned, the most influential skeptic in Mason's life was Miss Cassie, his shrink. He had an appointment with her today—too early, as usual—and he woke up already resenting her. Seeing her had become routine, and he kept going even though he wasn't always sure there was any tangible benefit. But if it was easy, he knew, he wouldn't be learning anything.

Forcing himself to sit up before he drifted off again, he rubbed his eyes and, despite the cold, rolled out of bed and pulled on a pair of boxers and a T-shirt. Ned was on the phone in the office, consumed with bankers and mortgage people. Mason waved, then went to the kitchen and fumbled with the espresso machine in his pre-caffeine stupor, finally getting it started. After he'd ingested most of the pot, he started another, and cut up some peaches and an Asian pear. He gulped down as much of the second pot as he could stomach and got dressed, long pants for a fall day, even though he knew it would warm up later.

Soon he was coasting down the hill to the boulevard, fallen leaves from the plane trees crunching under his tires, the brisk air dispelling the last of his morning brain fog. He carried his bike down the stairs into the metro station and was on his way downtown. Miss Cassie's building was a glammy art deco structure right across from the metro, and he loved climbing up out of the earth and admiring it on his way in. He locked up his bike and entered the lobby, restored to its 1930s splendor, complete with lofty murals and dark wood paneling. The elevator ride up to her floor led him back to the twenty-first century, as the office spaces were modern conversions with polished concrete floors and exposed brick.

The sliding sign on her door said COME IN, so he moved it to PLEASE KNOCK and went inside. Miss Cassie was at her desk, absorbed in her computer screen.

"Mason," she said, glancing up briefly. "Always a pleasure. Give me two minutes."

He pulled off his backpack and sat in his usual spot, under the tall windows with the towers of the financial district beyond. He enjoyed the view, just sitting and looking out while he waited. That alone almost made it worth the trip.

Miss Cassie came over and got comfortable in her chair, spending a minute on her tablet swiping through her notes before looking up and asking, "How are things going?"

He talked about his relationship with Ned and some of their other regular topics, Miss Cassie scribbling on her tablet with her stylus.

"And how's work?"

"I'm working, which is a good thing. I just got hired to hunt down a ghost."

"Interesting," she said. "Have you done that before?"

"I've never looked for one, or even seen one. I'm not really sure what they are, or if they even exist, to be honest. The upside is that I was actually able to talk frankly about it with Ned."

"What makes ghosts different than your other work?"

"I suppose it's because it's more common, less abstract."

"Let's revisit that," she said. "You lie to him about your other jobs, but you don't lie to me."

"You already think I'm crazy, so talking about my crazy experiences won't change our relationship."

"I never said I thought you were crazy," she said, looking up from her notes with a smile.

"I guess I feel like I'm protecting him, protecting the relationship. What he doesn't know won't hurt me."

"That might seem reasonable in the moment, when you're talking to him, but in the long run it will turn into a barrier." She watched him for a moment, tapping her stylus absently on the sofa cushion.

"Think outside your work," she said. "Would you tell Ned if you'd done something embarrassing?"

"Like what?"

"Losing some cash that you had in your pocket, for example, or tripping over the curb on a busy street."

"Of course I'd tell him," Mason said, furrowing his brow. "Things like that happen to me all the time."

"Would you tell him if you found another man attractive? Imagine you were out somewhere, in a restaurant or at the theater."

"Sure I would. Subtly, though—like, 'Hey, check out that guy.' I wouldn't drool."

"What if you made out with someone else, or slept with someone else?"

"I wouldn't do that."

"Why not?" She looked up at him. "If you're comfortable lying to him, he'd never know. What he doesn't know can't hurt him."

He laughed. "Miss Cassie, that's pretty dark for a woman of the church."

"I go to St. Agatha's for the community, not to make me blind to human nature."

"Well, I wouldn't do it, because *I'd* know. I couldn't live with that. Exercising a little self-control up front seems easier than all the crap that would come afterward."

"That's probably a good instinct," she said, resuming her notes for a moment, then glancing pointedly at the wall clock.

"Time to wrap it up, I suspect?" Mason said.

"It was a pleasure to see you, Mason. Let me leave you with something to consider: what's missing when you don't share everything with Ned?"

"I'll do that," he said, and took a minute to pull his notepad out of his backpack and write it down. He said good-bye and slid her door sign back to COME IN, then headed to the elevator.

Always the tough questions with her, he thought, riding down to the street. But she usually had a point.

He unlocked his bicycle and stood there for a minute, straddling it at the curb, to phone Matt, Peggy's boyfriend. He had originally been Mason's friend, a contact from the psychic world that Mason had set up with Peggy. So far, it seemed like his intuition had been right—things were working out between them. Matt wasn't a full-time psychic—he worked as a scientist in academia—but he had sharp skills, and Mason considered him a good resource.

"Are you around today?" Mason asked when he picked up. "Can I pick your brain?"

"It sounds like you're out on the street," Matt said. "Are you over at the library?"

Mason laughed. "Am I that predictable? I'm not far from there."

"I'm home. I'll meet you at that place over here— the one with the courtyard."

It wasn't far to cycle over to the Arts District, these days a tony retail and residential neighborhood long abandoned by any artist without a trust fund. Soon after he'd locked up his bike and found a table outside, Matt appeared.

"What up, motherfucker?" he said, dropping into the opposite chair. He was dressed in jeans and a sweatshirt, and from the looks of it hadn't shaved in a couple days.

"I heard you're going to a Peggy Pregnant concert," Mason said.

"Finally," Matt said emphatically. "Although I guess I should be grateful she asked me at all."

The waiter stopped at their table. "Gentlemen," he said. "What'll it be?"

"A triple espresso," Mason said, and Matt ordered a beer.

When the waiter had gone, Mason said, "You're obviously not headed to school today."

"Hell, no. It's midterms. I can forget about that place for a few days." He waved his arm. "So tell me about Peggy Pregnant."

"It's a whole thing. You'll see when you go. There are groupies, and they show up to every concert. No one ever talks about the pregnancy as fake. It's what she's bringing, and they accept it uncritically."

Matt nodded. "I can understand that. It's internally coherent."

"It's a little odd, but I always have a lot of fun."

"I'll let you know how it goes," he said. "So what did you want to talk about?"

Mason leaned forward, mentally shifting focus. "What are ghosts?" he asked.

"Well, they're not dead people, that's for damn sure."

"Thank you," Mason said emphatically, slapping the table.

The waiter set down his coffee cup and Matt's beer, hesitating momentarily to make sure Mason was done with his percussion.

Matt raised his glass and took a sip, then went on. "That's a pat explanation for a complex phenomenon, don't you think? Like how the sun revolved around the earth until the Greeks figured out what was really going on."

"It also doesn't mesh with what you and I know about time," Mason said, cradling his cup. They had met when Matt had slipped backward through time using his psychic skills and became stranded. Mason had helped pull him back, enlisted by a woman named Hanh. She ran a nail salon on Sunset Boulevard, but she could also move back and forth through time the way most people move between rooms.

"Speaking of that, have you heard from the boss lately?" Matt asked.

"Dude, do not call her that." After Hanh had recruited them to help her a second time, they were both concerned that she had some kind of supervisory role in the psychic world, and that she might be trying to deputize them.

Matt laughed. "You look worried."

"When you told me about the garuda character in mythology, I did some reading. It kind of fits. She could very well be one."

"The good news, though, is that she hasn't asked us to help her for a while."

Mason sipped at his coffee. "True," he said, but he wasn't so sure that meant they were off her radar.

"One theory that resonates with me," Matt continued, "is that ghosts are something to do with living people, not the dead. They're psychic projections, maybe, like astral travelers that you can see. But I have no idea how that works."

"I like that idea," Mason said. "It's so hard to get a handle on it because there's just so much noise about ghosts in the mainstream consciousness."

Matt nodded. "Look beyond all that."

"I used the astral projection technique when I was helping the engineer find ley lines," Mason said. "How could that relate to the ghost phenomena?"

"Imagine you astrally project your consciousness to my loft. You're not really there, just some part of your mind is. But maybe some people can sense your projection, and that's what we call ghosts. I might not know that it's you, but I see a glimmer, or hear something, or get a feeling that someone's there, so I think that my place is haunted."

"This is why I have to talk to you," Mason said. "You always make sense."

Matt grinned, flattered. "I'm glad someone thinks so."

They chatted a while longer, but Mason had things to do. He finished his coffee and left some cash with Matt, who was going to stay for another round, then headed out to the street.

Cycling back to the central library, he locked up his bike outside and detoured upstairs through the rotunda, for no other reason than to look up at the chandelier, a stained-glass representation of the earth ringed with lights. He'd seen it before, but it was so pleasant to look at something beautiful, even for a fleeting moment or two. He walked down the escalators to the history department, many floors below, and looked around for familiar faces among the staff, but none of the people he knew were there today.

Not far from the librarians' counter he found a desk and got settled, pulling out his computer and connecting to the library's catalog. He searched for "Montclair Security Building" and "suicide" but didn't come up with anything relating to Yoshida's property in Chinatown. Eventually, using other keywords, he found a newspaper article dated 1934. It was the only entry in the index that linked the building to the word *death,* and the time frame was right—it had to be what Yoshida's tenant had been talking about.

Some of the newspapers from the era had been digitized, but not the *Los Angeles Daily Bugle,* unfortunately; it still resided on microfilm, in discrete little boxes, inert and unseen by any but the most determined. Mason went to the counter and requested the appropriate spool, then got set up at a reader, balancing his computer on a corner of the bulky machine's worktable. Soon he was zooming through the long-ago pages of the newspaper, slowing down to check the date now and then, homing in on the right issue.

BODY FOUND AT MONTCLAIR SECURITY, the headline shouted from the front page. He scanned the article and learned what little was known. The dead woman was named Gladys Wright, and she had worked in the building as a clerk before being found by cleaners early on a Monday morning, sprawled on the floor in front of her desk. The cause of death was unclear, but the police were involved. A lurid photo accompanied the story, depicting a man in a broad-brimmed hat squatting beside a pair of feet shod in petite black lace-ups with chunky heels. Gladys's calves were visible, but the photo modestly ended partway up the rumpled gray skirt. "Assistant coroner examines the scene," explained the caption.

Mason sent the article to the printer, then turned to his computer and searched the database for a follow-up article. Surely the coroner had reported on the cause of death at some point soon afterward. But he couldn't find anything else with Gladys's name, or Montclair Security. There were several articles that year that mentioned the coroner's office, but only in relation to other deaths, nothing about Gladys. Perhaps the autopsy had determined a cause of death so mundane that it wasn't newsworthy. Maybe Peggy was right—the office job had sucked the life right out of her.

But there was also the possibility of a cover-up. Los Angeles local government was full of corruption, and the farther back in time you looked, the worse it got. It was easy to imagine that somebody who ran a profitable business like a security company could keep a story like that quiet if it had the potential to hurt their business. LA's history was rife with similar examples, where the rich and powerful insulated themselves from scandal by paying off prosecutors and law enforcement, to keep their names out of the courts and out of the news.

In any case, journalistic interest in Gladys seemed to have died with her that day. Maybe it didn't really matter, Mason decided, especially if he was working on the assumption that dead people didn't become ghosts—that would mean this case wasn't even about her. He'd hunted for Gladys's story because one of Yoshida's artists had mentioned it, but that person had based his tale on the same scant information about Gladys's death that Mason had. All he'd really learned was that that story hadn't been entirely fabricated.

He rewound the spool and returned it to the counter, picking up his printout and paying the librarian for it. Books about ghosts were kept on a different floor, and after taking a minute to figure out where they were, he folded his computer closed and stuffed it into his backpack. Trotting up the escalator, he soon found the shelves.

Like the tsunami of information online, there were a lot of books on the subject here, but at least they were better curated. With his head awkwardly turned sideways, he read the spines and pulled out a few volumes. One was a standard Western religious treatment from the mid-twentieth century, and another was a more recent rundown of Chinese ghosts. For the title alone, he had to take *Ghosts and Other Creatures Dispelled by the Piercing Beam of the*

Light of Science. It was even older than the religious book, written in the 1930s. Most exciting was *The Ghost as a Psychic Phenomenon,* with a scuffed and worn binding, but when he pulled it out and flipped it open, it turned out to have been published quite recently. He took the stack of books to a desk, then pulled his notepad out of his backpack so he could write down anything important.

The Western analysis talked about biblical ghosts, and Roman Catholic thought, and Spiritualism, a whole nineteenth-century Christian denomination built around contacting the spirits of the dead. He scanned a few other chapters, reading briefly about the idea that ghosts were dead people who had unfinished business in the world, but when the narrative turned to ghosts interpreted as demons, he folded it closed and set it aside.

The Chinese book was more engaging because the folklore was more nuanced. People who could see ghosts tended to be unlucky and unhappy in life, and people with good luck were oblivious to ghosts. Everyone, it seemed, became a regular ghost after death, some hanging around the earthly plane for a while, but people who suffered a lot in life or died violently became hungry ghosts—desperate creatures that were best banished through specific rituals. The overlap with the Western idea of spirits with unfinished business was interesting, but Yoshida hadn't said anything about his ghost's mission, just that it was noisy late at night.

The *Piercing Beam of the Light of Science* turned

out to be a range of ad hoc postulations tailored to explain away supernatural and fringe phenomena. Lake monsters were misinterpreted interference patterns in surface waves; the Jersey Devil, a livestock-eating monster from the East Coast that Mason had never heard of, was really a pack of sneaky woodland bobcats; and haunted buildings were actually troubled by unusual sound waves generated by boilers and factory equipment. That was Ned's explanation too—this author was clearly on the same skeptical wavelength.

A few minutes flipping through *The Ghost as a Psychic Phenomenon* told him he needed to take it home and actually read it rather than skimming for highlights. He slid his notepad into his bag and made his way to the automated checkout, where he scanned the volume, then pulled out his keys, swiping the little plastic library card on his key ring over the sensor. Stuffing the book into his backpack, he headed for his bike.

Half an hour later he was cycling up the hill to their house. Ned was still working in the office, and after saying hello to him and putting on a clean shirt, Mason stretched out on the sofa with his library book.

He hadn't noticed when he'd flipped through it before, but inside the front cover was a photo of the author, Marilyn Gaia. Shown from the waist up, she wore a dark robe with a cowl loose around her unruly hair, intently gazing at the camera with

a thin, knowing smile. In each hand she held a glass
ball, raised at either side of her head, the weight of
them splaying her hands outward. One sphere was
darker than the other, but it was hard to tell what
color they were in the black-and-white image. On
her robe, over her heart, embroidered in shiny thread
like a corporate logo on a pro athlete's jacket, was
the eye of Horus. The same icon figured prominently
on Mason's own business card. Is this what people
thought of him, a perplexing figure like Marilyn
Gaia, redolent of the occult? He sighed and flipped
the page.

Despite her dramatic portrait, Mason found
himself quickly pulled into Marilyn's explanation of
the ghost phenomenon. Her base assumptions paralleled his own understanding of the workings of the
world, and he was able to skip through some of the
familiar background material.

> What we perceive as ghosts are, in fact, strong projec-
> tions made by ordinary people using the astral body,
> either in daydreams or in the dream state. Often this
> happens unintentionally. Who among us does not
> have an emotional connection to a place—your child-
> hood bedroom, Mother's kitchen, a favorite teacher's
> classroom. When we daydream about these places,
> we may inadvertently appear there as a specter. These
> projections are not limited by geography, and some
> individuals manage to subconsciously send their astral
> bodies through time as well.

Repeated hauntings, Marilyn explained, were a
single projection smeared through time; to observers

it appeared to be multiple visits. It was unclear why ordinary people could detect the projections—could see and hear the ghosts—when most paranormal phenomena were evident only to those who had honed their senses, psychics like Marilyn. She theorized that projections were quite common, but the rare visible ones had changed frequency for some reason, like the Doppler effect or redshift in astronomy, moving it into the range perceptible by the ordinary senses.

It was fascinating stuff, and he got lost in the flow of reading. It made sense that the ghost phenomenon was another aspect of the paranormal world that he was familiar with, a window into other realms. He could discard the religious and folkloric explanations, he decided. Matt was right: they were misinterpretations. The piercing beam of science could go too—Marilyn's analysis made much more sense than vibrating ducts and pipes.

Ned came out from the office and dropped into an easy chair.

"Finished with work?" Mason asked him.

"Yeah," he said, and stretched back, arms reaching over his head, releasing the stress of the workday. "How about roasted squash for dinner?"

"I love it. Can I help you prep?"

"No, read your book. I'm going to decompress for a while first, but we'll eat in an hour."

Soon Ned was working in the kitchen, the smell of cooking gradually filling the house. Mason read through Marilyn's case studies, on various people who knew they had created a projection that was seen elsewhere and interpreted as a ghost. It was good reading, but he understood the theory without really needing the examples, and by the time Ned called him to eat he was finished with the book.

When he sat at the dining table, Ned set out a plate for him with half a squash, golden and glistening with maple syrup and dusted with herbs. The other half was on Ned's plate. He brought in two salads, then sat down.

"This looks amazing," Mason said. "Peggy isn't joining us?"

"She's got a gig, remember? Matt's introduction to Peggy Pregnant."

"Of course," Mason said. "I forgot. I saw him today. He seemed excited about it."

"What was his take on your haunting?"

"Well, he says that ghosts aren't dead people."

"Smart," Ned said, cutting a chunk off his squash. "I'd expect no less from a scientist. It's arrogant of us to think we persist beyond death."

"He thought they might be psychic projections, and this book I found says exactly that."

Ned sighed. "Projections from where?"

"Astral projections by living people. They aren't usually intentional, so people don't know they're doing it. Strong emotions can create them, even in the dream state."

"That sounds far-fetched," Ned said.

"But not scientifically impossible, right? One of the examples was this woman who used to daydream about the house she grew up in, on the other side of the country. One day she was back in that town, and she knocked on the door, and the person who lived there almost fainted. He said, 'You're the one who's been haunting my house.'"

"It's a great story, but it's not proof. That's the big mistake people make in woo-woo land: anecdotes aren't the same as reproducible evidence."

Mason took a breath before he responded. It wasn't a personal attack, he reminded himself. He pulled his salad plate closer and, struggling not to raise his voice, said, "It still makes more sense than a vibrating heating system. Doesn't that seem too contrived to cover all the ghosts that people see?"

"Maybe," Ned conceded. "But you know the thing about Occam's razor."

"Not really."

"It's a way to assess competing explanations. The one with the fewest assumptions is the most likely to be true."

"My explanation assumes more than yours?"

"Yes," Ned said emphatically. "Your version assumes a lot—astral projection, that's a big one."

"But it's not an assumption for me. I've done it, and I know people who've done it. To me the heating pipes thing seems more tenuous."

"OK, I get it," Ned said, looking away and setting down his fork. "So how was Miss Cassie today?"

"She actually thinks I should be more up-front with you about my work," Mason said, looking him in the eye.

Ned looked concerned. "Is there some part of it that you're not telling me?"

"I'm not hiding anything. But sometimes I leave out the more crazy-sounding stuff."

"I agree with Miss Cassie. You don't get to decide what I can handle and what I can't. I'd rather have the option to believe it or not."

"But you never believe it," Mason insisted. "That's the point."

"I can't help that," Ned said, raising his voice, gesturing widely.

"Well, I'm going to try to be more transparent," Mason said, pushing his empty plate away. "But it's hard to be on the receiving end of so much skepticism all the time."

"Another way to look at it is that it's not your job to protect me."

Mason nodded. He was right, and so was Miss Cassie. It wasn't a good pattern.

"Listen," Ned said, calmer now. "Since Peggy's out for the evening, we should get sexy."

Mason laughed. "I think getting me riled up turns you on."

"Your ears turn red, and your cheeks burn. Like I said before, fresh raspberries, just asking to be eaten. It is kind of hot."

"I'm glad you think so."

THREE

It was after midnight when Mason went back to the kitchen for a snack. He dug around in the fridge and found some pineapple that Ned had cut into chunks. Grabbing a fork, he took the container over to the French doors, where he stood and ate, looking out over the lights of the neighborhood.

He turned around when the front door opened. It was Peggy, bumping her unwieldy guitar case on the door frame, maneuvering it around her massive fake belly. She was still dressed for the stage, in a billowy maternity blouse and bell-bottom jeans, a band of daisies around her head.

"Hey, man," she said. "Sexy evening?"

"What?"

"You always wear those boxer shorts after you

two get busy, and you always come out for a snack."

"My god," Mason said. "I can't believe I'm that predictable."

"That's not necessarily a bad thing," she said, grinning at him and setting down her case, then pulling off her flowered headband.

"It's boring." He sat on the sofa and took another bite of pineapple. "Why don't you take off that outfit backstage instead of driving home in it?"

"I don't want my fans to see me unpregnant," she said, untying the belly behind her back and dropping it to the floor. "It would degrade my brand."

Seeing the belly on its own, detached from her body, always made him feel slightly nauseous. She'd bought it years ago at a film prop house bankruptcy sale, and there was really nothing sinister about it, but its odd organic shape was off-putting. He forced his eyes away.

Peggy sat across from him on an easy chair, sighing in relief, and kicked off her rattan wedges.

"How was it having Matt there?" he asked her.

"It went well. He seemed to enjoy himself, and he wasn't freaked out by the belly. He wanted to squeeze it to make sure it wasn't real."

Mason laughed. "So where is he? Aren't you two sleeping together yet?"

She frowned. "That's none of your damn business."

"Fair enough. I just figured, you were all up in my love life."

"I was, wasn't I," she said. "Actually, we are. But

I don't need to be sleeping over there. It's such a boy pad."

"I've never been to his place," Mason said.

"I worked all day, and then performing—I just want to sleep in my own bed." She massaged her temples. "How was your day?"

"I had coffee with Matt and asked him about ghosts. He had some good insights."

"So when are we going ghost hunting?" she asked.

"I've done my research, so whenever. It has to be after midnight, though."

She slapped the arm of the chair. "Let's go tonight."

"You just said you were tired."

"Not too tired for that. It's not going to take long, is it?"

"I don't think so," Mason said. "I'm thinking I'll just be poking around an empty building."

"We should go. It's in Chinatown?"

"Chinatown or Lincoln Heights, somewhere right around there. I have the address. It's not far." He hadn't planned it for tonight, but he appreciated her enthusiasm. And she had a car, so he wouldn't have to navigate there on two wheels in the middle of the night.

"I'll change," she said, and headed for her room, new energy in her step.

Mason followed her down the hall. Ned looked comfortable in bed, reading a novel by the light of his bedside lamp. Mason explained what he was doing and pulled open his side of the closet.

"Black pants for ghost hunting?" he asked.

"It doesn't matter what you wear," Ned said flatly. "They're not real, and you're going to an empty building."

"I'm thinking black pants," Mason said, and chose a black polo shirt too. He pulled on his thin-soled sneakers, since they were stealthy on hard floors.

Peggy came to the bedroom door, still wearing her voluminous stage blouse, sagging to her knees without its stuffing. "Ooh, ninja style," she said, assessing Mason's outfit. "Should I wear something dark, like you, or camo?"

"Not camo. We're not robbing a bank," Mason said. "And if we both wear black, we'll look like Kraftwerk."

"Never heard of them."

"You lie," he said. "Face facts, Peggy: no computers, no music."

"Flannel, then, I think," she said, ignoring him and heading back to her room.

"It's not going to matter," Ned called after her, exasperated. "The ghosts don't care, because they're not real."

Mason leaned down to kiss him good-bye. "We won't be long."

"Take a flashlight," Ned said. "There's a little one in the junk drawer."

"Good idea." He went into the kitchen to find it, then shoved it into his pants pocket and followed Peggy out the front door. She had chosen a red plaid top and jeans.

"You look like you're ready to work," Mason said, climbing into the passenger seat of her Prius.

"If we have to move furniture or operate heavy machinery, I'm ready," she said, starting the car and nosing down the hill toward the boulevard.

It was just a few miles away, but when he punched the address into his phone, it said the freeway was the fastest route at this hour.

"Do we have to tell your client that we're going in?" Peggy asked.

"He said I could stop by whenever. There's no one there—they all moved out—so it won't matter."

"Are you nervous?" she asked.

"Not really, because I don't think there's any danger." He explained Marilyn Gaia's theories about projections.

"If that's true, what are we hunting?" she asked, accelerating up the ramp onto the freeway.

"I figured I'd use my psychic skills to see more than just the visible part of the projection. Maybe I can figure out where it originates."

Moments later they were off the freeway and following the directions on his phone through the dark streets of an old industrial area.

"This is where all the rail yards are," Peggy said, dubiously surveying the factory fences topped with razor wire, the lifeless loading docks. "I thought you said it was in Chinatown. This isn't Chinatown, Mason."

"It's close, though. Yoshida called it North Chinatown," he said, peering out the window. "That's it."

He pointed to a hulking brick facade on the right.

Peggy pulled up in front, the lone car on the block, and turned off the ignition.

"Atmospheric," she said finally, leaning forward to look at the building through the windshield.

"Come on," Mason said. "It'll be fun." He climbed out onto the sidewalk and closed the car door, then looked over the structure. Dim light was visible from inside through the bars on the windows, set high above the street. Along the top in faded paint he could make out the words MONTCLAIR SECURITY.

"How do we get in?" Peggy asked, stepping around the front of the car and eyeing the heavy steel door.

"There's a lockbox," Mason said, scanning the door and the shallow steps leading up to it.

"Is this it?" she asked, pointing out a black key box, the kind real estate agents use, attached to a pipe near the door.

"It must be," Mason said, flipping up the cover to reveal the keypad. "What's your birthday again?" he asked, looking back to her.

"You know when my birthday is," she said, keeping her voice low despite the absence of any sign of life nearby.

"Just say the numbers."

"Why? You know it's October twenty-fourth."

"Does that make you a Taurus?" he asked, furrowing his brow.

"Are you kidding me? What kind of a psychic are you?"

Mason laughed. "Not the kind who uses astrology."

He turned back to the keypad and recited the numbers as he punched them in. "One, zero, two, foe. Peggy is a Scorpio," he chanted, pulling the box open and plucking out the key with a flourish.

"That was weird," she said. "Did you give that number to Yoshida?"

"No—he gave it to me. It's just a coincidence." He slid the key into the lock and twisted it. The deadbolt moved out of the way with a muted *thunk.*

"You always say there are no coincidences."

"Then I guess it's significant that you're here," he said, grinning at her and pulling on the door handle. It didn't budge—it was still locked.

"There's a lock in the handle too," she said, stepping closer to take a look.

"But there's only one key," Mason said, holding it up to show her.

"It's probably the same key for both locks," she said. "Try it."

He did, and it twisted freely, unlocking the handle.

"What did I tell you?" he said. "That's the reason you're here—to show me how doors work."

She chuckled. "You should put the key back in the box."

"Why?" Mason asked, pausing on the threshold.

"So that we don't forget it. You don't need it to get out, see? The deadbolt is a thumb lock on the inside."

He dutifully put the key back in the lockbox and snapped it shut while Peggy held the door open.

In the foyer, thankfully the lights were on. A hallway led toward the back of the building and a flight of stairs going up. As Yoshida had warned him, the place was rough. The office doors had all been taken off, and few patches of linoleum remained, mostly torn up to reveal mottled concrete. The erstwhile offices had blotchy and fading decades-old paint, boxy shadows remaining where furniture had once covered the walls. The windows were opaque with grime and slotted with heavy security bars.

"Gross," Peggy said quietly, looking into one space, then another. "I hope he wasn't charging people very much to work in here."

Mason walked toward the back of the building. In a little room beside the fire exit he found an electrical breaker box. Peggy was close behind him.

"Ned said to look for this," he said. "Turn off the power, he said, and the ghosts go away."

"Maybe we should wait until we actually see a ghost. If you turn it off now, you won't know whether that technique works."

"Good point."

"Did you notice the air vents?" she asked. "They're in every room. That means it's forced-air heating. That could also be the source of the sound."

"In Ned's mind, at least," he said.

"I'm not surprised someone thought this place was haunted," she said. "It's a little spooky."

"We should go up to the second floor. That's where the tenants said they heard something— room 203."

They went back to the foyer and trudged up the stairs. Mason stepped into the first office at the top—only to be confronted by a woman holding a baseball bat. He quickly recoiled, holding up his hands. This was no specter—she was a few feet away, toward the back of the room, but very real, and she was poised to swing.

"Back off, Stretch," she snapped. "I'm armed."

"Whoa," Mason said, bumping into Peggy as he took a step back.

"Ow," Peggy complained.

"I'm working for Yoshida," Mason said, eyes wide.

"The landlord?" the woman said, tentatively lowering the bat. "What are you doing here?"

He stared at her, breathing hard to dispel the flood of adrenaline. "An inspection."

"In the middle of the night?" she asked, frowning.

"It's an inspection for ghosts," Peggy said, stepping around him and into the room. "We represent a psychic investigation agency, and we're here late because that's when the unusual activity was reported."

Her amicable tone seemed to set the woman at ease. Calming down, Mason realized she had to be one of the tenants. A couple of boxes sat near the doorway, loaded with small blank canvases, stained brushes, metal tools. She looked like an artist too, in a loose tank top, paint-stained jeans, her hair in a natural Afro. Around the base of her neck was a dark tattoo in swirling decorated script, but he couldn't make out what it said.

"You were renting space here?" he asked. "Yoshida said you'd all moved out."

"I'm leaving now," she said. "I just needed to get the last of my stuff." She nodded at the boxes. "Sorry about the bat," she said to Peggy, setting it on top of one of her boxes. "I keep it nearby in case the ghost isn't just a ghost."

"Have you seen it?" Peggy asked.

"It's a she. I've only heard her, but one of the guys who worked here actually saw her. He said she was all gray."

"What did you hear?" Mason asked.

"A voice talking, when I knew no one else was in the building, and sometimes a machine sound. It's like a power saw, or a rotary grinder. High-pitched, but with a wobble in it, a vibration. It's completely unnerving."

"How do you know it's not someone working next door, or out on the street?" Peggy asked.

She arched her thin-plucked eyebrows. "Because it's loud, and it's not muffled. If the sound was coming through the walls it would lose all the higher frequencies. It sounds like it's in the next room, but when you go to look, there's nothing there."

"Is it always coming from the same place?" Mason asked.

She nodded. "At the back, on the left. Room 203." Her phone chimed, and she pulled it out of her pants and glanced at the screen. "That's my ride," she said. "You'll have to excuse me."

Mason stood aside as she heaved up one of the

boxes and carried it down the stairs. Peggy raised her eyebrows and nodded to the other box.

"What?" he asked her, and then figured it out. He picked up the other box and took it down, handing it to the woman. She loaded it into the trunk of an idling car.

"Thanks," she said. "Tell Yoshida I'm completely out of here, and I won't be back."

Peggy was at the front door, holding it open. They went back inside as the car drove away.

"Did you see her collar tattoo?" she asked. "It was huge."

"That is not going to be pretty when she's eighty-five. Could you read it?"

"It said 'Only God can judge me.' You know who has tats like that?"

"Artists?"

"Strippers, and prostitutes, and gangbangers. People who have done something they think others will judge them for."

"She didn't look like any of those things," Mason said, glancing up the stairs apprehensively. "Although it's hard to tell."

"She might be an artist, but there's something else going on. I don't judge, but she could totally be a hooker."

"We should probably check out all the rooms. Should we split up?"

"No way. I'm sticking with you."

They went into each office on the ground floor, glancing around. Mason wasn't quite sure what he was looking for. Some of the rooms had ceiling lights but others were lit only by the light from the hallway, so he pulled out the flashlight and cast the beam around. Aside from crumpled paper, stained paint rags, and other creative debris, there was nothing but empty space.

Back in the foyer, Mason said, "Maybe I'll try to read the place," waggling his fingers to put air quotes around "read."

"Is that a delaying tactic so you don't have to go into that room upstairs?" Peggy asked.

"No—I'll get there. It's just a preliminary step." He looked around and decided to sit on the stairs. "I'll need complete silence."

Peggy laughed. "I'll get right on it, chief." She stepped back to give him some space, but didn't go too far.

Mason closed his eyes and cleared his mind, imagining his awareness was expanding outward to encompass the building. He waited for some feeling or insight to filter in, some sense of who was projecting the ghostly image to this place. The photo of Gladys's lifeless calves flashed into his mind. He wondered what room that had happened in, where the coroner had been squatting and examining the body, but then he pushed it away. It was a memory of the newspaper article, not an insight. As he concentrated on nothingness again, slowly an image formed— green fields, rolling hills, the countryside in summer. It was idyllic, and calming, and he made a mental note to write it down later for the case file, but it didn't seem to have anything to do with projections or ghosts.

He opened his eyes and sighed. "Nada," he said, and got to his feet.

He was about to mount the stairs when they heard it—a high-pitched whine, building gradually in volume. It was just as the artist had described it, the sound of a high-speed motor with distortion or wobble in it. He looked at Peggy, whose eyes had grown wide.

"Where is it coming from?" she said under her breath.

"I can't tell. Does it seem like it's upstairs?"

They stood listening, and the sound suddenly dropped off, replaced by voices—a woman's, but also a man's, having an ordinary conversation—but he couldn't make out what they were saying. It was clear now where the sound was coming from, however: upstairs.

"Cut the power," Peggy said suddenly.

"Good thinking." Mason walked toward the back of the building as quietly as he could, heart pounding, Peggy close behind him. He flipped the main breaker, plunging them into darkness, then pulled out the flashlight and switched it on. They stood there, the sharp white circle of light on the floor between them, and listened. For a second he thought it had silenced the voices, but no, he could still hear them. They were fainter back here, but they were still talking, calm and businesslike. He walked to the foyer to make sure.

"One strike for Ned," Peggy said.

"I think we have to go upstairs. Let me get the lights." He went back and flipped the breaker, illuminating the building, then switched off his flashlight.

"This is freaking me out," Peggy whispered when he stepped back into the hall. She took the flashlight from his hand, even though the lights were back on, and turned it off and on absently. "Should we go?"

"I'm scared too, but I'm trying to be rational," he whispered back. When he paused, the voices were still audible. "I think I have to go up and look. You can stay here—"

"No," she hissed. "I'll be right behind you. Just don't back up too quickly. I only have eight unbroken toes left."

He started up the staircase, treading lightly so as not to make any noise. The voices were definitely coming from the back of the building, on the left— room 203. He walked down the hall from the top of the stairs, feeling his heartbeat accelerating. The voices were louder now, pausing in conversation then resuming again. He still couldn't make out the words, just the murmur of speech.

Room 203 was definitely the source of the sound. As he came up to it, light was spilling out of the doorway—crisp white, more like his flashlight than like Yoshida's dingy yellow ceiling fixtures. Taking a deep breath, he stepped inside, half expecting to see Gladys's gray figure.

Instead, there was a lighted sphere, about five feet across. At first Mason thought it was flat, projected on the wall, but no—it was floating in the middle of the room. Strangest of all, it seemed three-dimensional, with edges that were indistinct, rippling. He stepped closer, and his perspective changed. He could see into it, he realized, *through* it—it was a disk-shaped hole into another room, much bigger than this one, and brightly lit. The floor wasn't quite level with the one he was standing on, so everything looked tilted, like a photo taken at a slight angle. He could see three people, a woman and two men, wearing lab coats, sitting behind a console a few yards inside the hole.

"It's stabilized," one of the men said.

Mason stared in wonder. He felt Peggy at his elbow.

"What the hell?" she said, no fear in her voice now.

The woman at the console peered out at them, and a look of alarm came over her face. "There are gangsters in there," she shouted. "Shut it down—now!"

Both men quickly scrambled into action, one of them jabbing at the console, panicked and flailing. The high-pitched mechanical whine filled the room again, almost unbearably loud, and the sphere of light suddenly shrank to a point and disappeared, along with the noise.

Mason and Peggy stood there for a moment, silenced by shock, staring at the empty office, now like the others, containing nothing more exotic than ancient fading paint.

"They heard you," Mason said finally. "They could see us."

"What was that?" Peggy asked. "It certainly wasn't

a ghost." She stepped carefully across the room, through the place where the sphere had been, waving her arms as if to check whether it was completely gone.

"It wasn't a psychic projection either. At least not the kind the ghost book talked about."

"They looked kind of ... science-y," she said. "And they were speaking English."

"Did she call us gangsters?" he asked, going through it in his mind as the astonishment faded.

"She was looking right at us as she said that, so yeah, she meant us."

"Why would she say that?"

"More important, who were they? *Where* were they?"

"No idea," he said, "but it didn't feel psychic at all. It felt ..."

"Real," Peggy said. "I saw it as plainly as you did. It was objectively real."

He nodded. Peggy was right—it had been real. His excitement grew, and he could feel it in his stomach. This is why he did this work, the psychic research—there was nothing like this mind-boggling feeling of wonder.

"We should get out of this crazy place," she said. "But first I have to pee. Did you see a restroom?"

"Right at the top of the stairs." Mason had noticed the antique porcelain fixtures and ancient tile as they walked by.

"You have to come with me. And you have to wait outside."

It was just a few steps to the restroom. He leaned on the wall outside as she went in and closed the door. He understood her instinct—it did feel safer to stay together. He was glad she'd come with him. As he waited, he ran through his mind again what they'd seen, the people, and how they'd reacted, wishing he'd brought a notepad to write it all down.

"This is the nicest room in the building," she called to him through the door.

Suddenly the high-pitched whine started again. Mason snapped upright and looked back toward room 203. A white glow emanated from the doorway—it was happening again. Peggy either didn't hear it or was too startled to speak. It wouldn't hurt to leave her alone for a few seconds—she was safe in the restroom, after all.

He walked back to the office doorway and looked in. Again the sphere filled the middle of the room, but this time the edges were strobing, shrinking by an inch or so, then rebounding. As he walked around it, the interior came into focus. He found he was looking into the same room again, with the console, white walls, and a high ceiling. He stepped closer to get a better look, and stood still, taking it all in. The polished floor was even more slanted than before, and the people at the console looked different. There were only two of them, a man and a woman. The guy had been there before, although now he wasn't wearing a lab coat. The woman was the same too, he decided, after watching her for a moment.

She looked up and caught his eye, but she didn't react this time.

"We've got an artifact," she said.

The man looked up at Mason. "Are you sure he's not real?"

"He's static, Blanchard," she said, irritation in her tone. "Real people move around. It's an artifact, caught between frames."

Blanchard's eyes narrowed as he peered at Mason. "I guess you're right." He scoffed. "Looks like a bona fide twenty-first-century orangutan."

Mason felt the color rise to his cheeks. He heard it every day, so he should be used to it: "Red," "Ginger," "Agent Orange." He shouldn't react, he knew that, but he couldn't help himself.

"It takes an orangutan to know an orangutan, you hairball," he said loudly. The guy actually had great hair, wavy and enviably stylish without being too coiffed, but there was a lot of it, and Mason couldn't think of any other insult to hurl at him.

The pair froze. Before they could move, in a split second Mason made a rash decision—he stepped over the edge of the sphere and into their space.

FOUR

"Who's an orangutan now, Blanche?" Mason said, trying to lock eyes with Blanchard, but it was like stepping into a fun house with an uneven floor, and he lost his footing on the first step, tumbling sideways onto his butt.

Blanchard screamed and slapped at the console. Mason looked back through the sphere, into room 203, dark and empty, where he should be—he needed to jump back in there. Before he could even get to his feet, the familiar high-pitched whine shrieked on and off, and the sphere collapsed into itself, shrinking to nothing like a burst soap bubble. He was staring instead at the bank of machinery behind it, racks of indecipherable shiny components, taller than he was and filling half the room.

He turned toward the console.

"Stay away," the woman snapped, stepping backward, even though Mason hadn't moved.

"Send him back," Blanchard pleaded.

"We can't," the woman shouted, angry now. "You turned off the machine."

"Security!" Blanchard shouted, cowering behind the console, fearful eyes locked on Mason. He didn't seem to have a phone or a radio, but said, "A gangster got through. He might be armed."

"Are you talking about me?" Mason asked. Neither of them replied, and he watched them for a minute. Finally he got to his feet. Both of them flinched, and Mason held up both palms, speaking as calmly as he could. "I'm not armed. I'm not going to hurt anybody."

A set of doors swung open in the far wall, behind the console, and two guys in identical outfits stepped in. Mason didn't recognize the uniforms, the odd little hats with a narrow brim in front, but that officious shade of blue was unmistakable—these were cops.

You idiot, he berated himself. Why did you do that? One thoughtless misstep, and now he was getting arrested.

In sharp contrast to the pair at the control panel, the cops were completely calm—not disinterested, not overly authoritative, but almost perfunctory.

"What's going on, Annette?" the older one asked, stopping at the console but keeping an eye on Mason. It made sense that the woman was the boss; she was older than Blanchard.

"He wasn't supposed to, but he got through," she

said. "It was just a calibration run. We thought he was an artifact."

The younger cop hung back at the console, a plain laboratory fixture that was undeniably tangible, but the other one walked past it toward the machinery and Mason. "I don't think he's armed," he said.

"I have no weapons," Mason said, meeting his eye and keeping his voice even.

"Sensors got nothing," the younger cop said, although he wasn't looking at a sensor or a screen. He was just standing there, arms folded, watching Mason.

"I'm not going to hurt you," the older cop said, smiling faintly and moving closer.

"I get it," Mason said, raising his arms instinctively. He knew he had no choice but to surrender.

The guy was several inches shorter than Mason, with a slight build, so he wasn't physically intimidating, but he quickly went to work frisking him. He felt under his arms, wasn't shy about thoroughly groping his crotch, and then ran his hands down his pant legs. He pulled Mason's phone out and looked at the front and back, not turning the screen on, and then slipped it back in the pocket where he'd found it. He pulled out Mason's key ring and examined the little plastic card with the bar code on it. It was jarring to see his keys, so much a part of his ordinary life that he almost ignored them, but so alien in this room, just like he was.

"Los Angeles Public Library," the cop read aloud, and dropped the keys back into Mason's pants.

Finally he stepped back and looked him over, frowning slightly, sizing him up. "Well," he said, turning toward the others, "it looks like it works. Your test subject is alive, in one piece, and lucid."

"He's not a test subject," Annette said. "That's years away."

Mason wanted to ask her what was going on, who she was, where he was—but he knew it was probably wiser to let the situation cool off first. This was most definitely a real place, and these were real people. He had to demonstrate he was willing to cooperate.

The younger cop turned on his heel and walked out the door without a word. It was a good sign, Mason thought, that things might be deescalating.

"Why would you think I was a gangster?" he asked. "I'm not going to hurt anyone."

"I know," the cop said, smiling reassuringly.

Annette was still looking at Mason dubiously, although she seemed calmer, probably because the cop's search hadn't turned up anything. "He doesn't look like he's from the 1950s," she said.

Did she think that was where he was from? It was worrisome, because it meant that more than just stepping into another room, he may have stepped into another era. What were these people up to? More concerning right now, though, was that she was talking about him like he was a piece of furniture. He needed to connect with her, with all of them, if he wanted to be treated like a human being, and have any hope of getting out of here. "I'm standing right here," Mason said to her firmly. "I do speak English."

"That's the *other* one," Blanchard said, still upset. "This is the newer one."

"You brought someone else through?" the cop asked, looking from Blanchard to Annette. "That's news to me."

"Not another person," Blanchard said, exasperated. "The other target."

"I see," the cop said. He looked to Mason and shrugged. "It's all way above my head."

"Don't go blabbing about our proprietary secrets," Annette said to Blanchard.

"That's why Qualtrough bailed," Blanchard replied, his lip curling into a sneer. "You are always riding us."

"I already know you've ripped holes in reality," Mason said, raising his voice before she could reply. "It's not really a secret from me, if that's what you're worried about."

She stared at him, as if realizing he was sentient for the first time.

"It's not even all that exotic," Mason continued, holding her gaze while he had her attention. "Your porthole traverses time, does it not? I can bleed through time too. Although I don't punch holes in it with technology," he said, looking at the racks of equipment.

Annette scoffed. "Sure you can. It's not possible without these machines."

"Now who's blabbing?" Blanchard said, but she ignored him.

"I know lots of people who can," Mason replied.

55

"There are rules, though, and we're discreet."

"Impossible," she said, folding her arms.

"You're doing it, but I can't?" Mason said. He looked to the cop and grinned. "Science is the height of arrogance."

The cop gestured widely, as if to say, "He's got a point," and looked back to Annette.

"Listen," Blanchard said. "What are we going to do?"

"Let me go back," Mason said quickly. "Turn on your machine, and I'll be on my way."

"It has to run through a cycle to recharge," Annette said. "That takes about eighteen hours. You're here for a while."

His heart sank. He'd left Peggy alone in that building. She'd be freaked out that he was gone. He felt a twinge of sadness at being apart from Ned too, knowing he'd be worried. But at least it sounded like Annette was willing to send him back.

"In that case, can I get some food until then? And some sleep?"

"I can help with that," the cop said cheerfully. He gestured toward the doors.

Mason hoped that didn't mean he was going to jail, but it seemed likely. It would be the logical thing to do with a trespasser. He resigned himself to it—his only way out of here was by cooperating with these people. Why had he stepped through? He chastised himself mentally. Walking ahead of the cop, he passed the console, eyeing Annette and Blanchard. Their alarm at his presence had worn off, but they watched him intently.

When he reached the door he grabbed the handle and twisted it, but it was locked. He turned back to the cop, who was a few paces behind him. A voice spoke from somewhere overhead.

"Would you kindly identify yourself?" it asked, polite but firm.

It sounded a lot like natural speech, but it was too smooth. It had to be generated by software.

"It's OK," the cop said, looking at the door rather than toward the source of the voice. "He's in my custody."

"He's not chipped," the voice said.

"Let me worry about that," the cop said.

Something inside the lock clicked softly, and Mason tried the handle again. It opened freely this time. They left the room, and the cop walked beside him, guiding him through a maze of institutional corridors. It felt like a college, or a sprawling office building.

"So where are we?" Mason asked.

"On the way to the cafeteria," the cop said tersely, clearly not amenable to being quizzed.

They passed a couple of other lab-coated people on the way, and they looked at Mason curiously, but didn't seem overly concerned. It didn't feel like he was in custody. Despite discouraging conversation, the cop was relaxed, tapping him gently on the arm when he missed a turn.

That door was odd, he thought, controlled by a talking computer that was smart enough to defer to the cop when pressed. The wall of tech in that big room was unfamiliar too, maybe even futuristic. Blanchard had mentioned the machine connecting to the past. It all implied the same thing, he realized—this was the future.

Finally they came to another vast room, the cafeteria, with food cases along one side and tables and chairs filling the floor space. There were a few people scattered around, some in lab coats and some not, but it wasn't busy. Most impressive was that one full wall, at least two stories high, was windows—the first glimpse he'd had outside the building. The view was dramatic, of green rolling lawns in front with a forested hill rising off to the right.

Above the horizon was the distinctive pink band that the eastern sky takes on at sunset. It was too green to be anywhere near LA, and it was a completely different time of day than when he'd left. It was possible that they were in another part of the world, but everyone he'd met spoke English the way he did. They were Americans.

"Nice," Mason said, pausing to admire the view.

The cop chuckled. "We think so."

Mason took a tray and perused the food offerings, stopping at the pastry case.

"Is there someone who works here?" he asked, looking around. "I wonder if any of these are vegan."

The cop frowned. "They all are."

"Sweet," Mason said, and took a brioche and two Danishes. Whatever this place was, it was certainly progressive. He poured himself a coffee and carried the tray to the end of the counter.

"How do I pay?" he asked, pulling his wad of cash out of his pocket.

"Is that a sawbuck?" the cop asked, taking the bills from Mason's hand and poring over them, smiling faintly, rubbing the paper between his fingers, holding it up to the light.

"Does that mean a ten-dollar bill?" he asked. He thought he'd heard the word before, but it sounded antiquated.

The cop handed the cash back. "You don't have to pay. It's all included here."

"Where is 'here'?" Mason asked. "Is this a university? It kind of feels like one. What city are we in?"

"It's a research institute," the cop said, meeting Mason's eye and again tacitly shutting down his questions. He gestured to a table, and Mason sat facing the windows, self-consciously nibbling on the brioche as the cop sat opposite, watching him.

"So what's your name?" he began, a pleasant smile on his face.

The cop was being exceedingly polite, but Mason knew it was a tactic to disarm him. The overture of friendship, even the suggestion of shared experience back in the lab, were masterful ways to build trust and get to the truth. He was under no illusion that this was anything other than an interrogation.

"Mason Braithwaite."

"And what's your street name?"

He frowned. "I don't have one of those."

"What do people call you?"

"Mason." He sipped at his coffee and asked, "What's your name?"

"Louie Louie. But everyone just calls me Louie."

Mason wanted to ask if his mother had given him that name, but he held his tongue. It was no weirder than anything else that had happened in the last few hours.

"Where are you from, Mason?"

"Los Angeles."

"Nice," Louie said, nodding. "I was out there last winter."

"So this isn't anywhere near LA," Mason said, looking around the room.

Louie didn't respond, but asked, "What do you do?"

"I'm a psychic investigator. Missing persons, property crime, intractable mysteries. I don't do boy-girl stuff."

He laughed. "That's quite a career." And more seriously, "Have you ever been arrested or charged with a crime?"

He shook his head. "I've had plenty of dealings with you people, but I never got arrested."

"Why do you have a public library bar code on your keys?"

Mason frowned, and set down his brioche. "Because I use the library?"

"That's logical." Louie nodded and watched Mason for a minute, then looked away. "Mr. Blanchard," he said, and paused, staring into space.

"Are you talking to me?" Mason asked, confused.

Not looking at him, Louie held up a finger.

"I've completed my investigation," he continued. "You can't leave your guest alone in the cafeteria."

Mason heard faint whispering, but couldn't parse the words. It was the other side of the conversation, he realized. Louie must be talking into a headset that Mason couldn't see.

"There is no threat," Louie said, turning in his chair and looking out the windows. "I've got other things to do. I'm not going to babysit." Looking back to Mason, he smiled and said, "See you later."

"Are you talking to me now?" Mason demanded.

"Of course." Louie got up to leave.

"Wait," Mason said. "What am I supposed to do?"

"Mr. Blanchard will be here presently. Enjoy the evening." He turned and walked toward the corridor.

Mason watched him leave, and a smile spread across his face. It was great news that Louie had lost interest in him—a huge relief. It meant he wasn't going to spend the night in the hoosegow. He wasn't sure how the guy had determined so quickly that Mason wasn't a security risk. Maybe he was good at spotting deception, and Mason hadn't needed to lie to him.

He started into a Danish and stared out the window. It was almost dark, the last of the deep blue sky giving way to black around the horizon. Louie had acted oddly—he hadn't been wearing an earpiece, at least not visibly, but he'd definitely made a call. Maybe the phone was implanted in his skull. Or maybe it was so futuristic, it was invisible.

Finishing his last pastry, decidedly classical in its

shape and flavor, he looked around at the other diners, some alone, some chatting in twos and threes. Nothing about them looked like science fiction, although their clothing was uniformly bland, like casual Friday at a big conservative company. But there was something different about this place. He thought about it, and looked around at the tables, the food cases, trying to pin it down. There were no TVs, that was part of it. And no piped music—just low conversations at other tables.

As the stress of his predicament subsided, he felt tired, and stood up to get another coffee. On his way back from the dispenser he spotted Blanchard, headed toward him. He looked worried, walking quickly, his jaw taut.

Mason sat down and gestured amicably to the other chair. Blanchard sat with him, but he didn't speak, instead eyeing him nervously. Lots of science people had atrophied social skills, Mason knew, but it was hard not to be resentful that he was going to have to break the ice, do the heavy lifting—especially when this was the guy whose trash talk had goaded him into this mess in the first place.

"Blanchard," Mason said, feigning familiarity. "What kind of name is that?"

"It's my name," he said, looking confused. "It's a family name."

"I know that. Is your family Brazilian?"

"It's possible. Maybe way back. Why do you ask?"

"You've got the whole Latin and African thing going on. I've heard it called the Brazilian mix."

Blanchard scowled and shifted in his chair. "Race works differently now."

Clearly Mason had offended him. He changed tack, dropping the camaraderie. "When is now, anyway? I know your stupid machine burrowed through time."

"It's not stupid."

"You talked about the 1950s, and you called me a twenty-first-century orangutan."

"And you called me Blanche," Blanchard said, meeting his eye.

"I did. So is this not the twenty-first century?"

"We're not that far apart," Blanchard said, averting his gaze.

"I know it's far. You all have invisible cell phones, and I got interrogated by a door."

"Cell phones?" Blanchard repeated, his brow furrowing.

"You're dodging my question. Is it because of Annette's whole thing about proprietary information?"

He nodded. "It's more than proprietary. It's classified."

Mason thought for a moment, taking a sip from his coffee cup. "You can't deny that I'm already in the middle of your classified stuff. Dude, it's in my field. I know what you created with your technology. I stepped through your porthole, and you saw me do it."

"We call it a portal," he said. "I can't tell whether you're mispronouncing that, or whether you're saying 'port hole.'"

"I don't care what you call it," Mason said, unable to suppress his frustration.

Blanchard looked startled, and then looked away, embarrassed.

"Can you at least tell me where we are? Is that classified?"

"Not far from Burlington, Vermont."

"That explains why the lawn is so green," Mason said, half to himself. "But you can't say when."

"Is it that important?" he asked. "You're leaving again tomorrow."

"That's definitely my priority," Mason said, glad to hear him say it.

"I don't think you should know, in case it changes something when you go back."

"I'd be shocked if reality was so fragile," Mason said, but he didn't press it. What was truly significant was that they planned to send him back. That was very good news. He sipped his coffee and looked at the wall of windows, now completely black with the darkness outside.

"I'm curious about something you said, Mason. You claim this is your field, and that you can move through time on your own. Is that part of your psychic practice?"

"Who told you I was a psychic?" Mason asked, frowning. "Come to think of it, I don't think I told you my name either."

"You told Louie," Blanchard said impatiently. "I heard a summary."

"When? I just talked to him."

"I wondered if it was a psychic ritual, or some kind of belief," he said, ignoring the question. "Or is it drug-induced?"

"It's not a religious thing," Mason said. "And it's not a hallucination. Why would you think that?"

"We've done extensive research. We know it's impossible to move in time without our technology. It's the only system of its kind."

"What's impossible is your myopia," Mason said, color rising to his face. "You sound just like your boss. There's more going on in the world than you think there is, even with your talking doors and your stupid temporal hole-punch."

Blanchard held up his palms. "Don't get upset. Can you just tell me why you think you can move through time? How does it work?"

Mason sighed. "I can slip into the past and then back to the present, just by thinking about it, focusing on it the right way. Other psychics call it a bleed-through. Sometimes it feels more like that, like I'm seeing the past but I'm not really there. Other times, I'm really there."

"Can you bleed into the future?"

"No—and I'm not sure if it's some kind of rule, or if it's just a psychological barrier for me personally. I'm fairly new at it."

"How far can you go?"

"Not far. I went forty years the first time I did it, and I had to be rescued."

"By who?" Blanchard asked, his eyes alive with curiosity, like a child's. At least his initial reticence had faded.

"My boyfriend's manicurist, Hanh. I'm sure that sounds crazy. I think she's more than that, though—one of my colleagues says she's a garuda."

Blanchard raised his eyebrows expectantly.

"It's from Asian mythology. A birdlike entity that supervises paranormal activity."

"So she's mythological, but she came to help you? How do you distinguish between mythology and reality?"

"I have no idea," Mason said, gesturing help-lessly. "My understanding of reality gets murkier by the day."

"Such an interesting story."

He murmured assent. Clearly Blanchard didn't believe any of it. Mason had seen that blank wall before, most often in Ned. The easiest way to deal with it was to let it be.

"You look tired," Blanchard said.

Mason nodded. "It's the middle of the night where I came from."

"I'll take you to a guest room."

They rose, and Mason followed him back into the corridor, up a flight of stairs, and through another maze of hallways.

"This place is huge," he said.

"There's a lot of room," Blanchard agreed. "Some of us stay here, and some stay off-campus."

Mason didn't ask all the questions that ran through his head: who "us" was, what the campus was, how many people worked here. He knew Blanchard was determined not to say much.

Finally they stopped in front of a door, and Blanchard pushed it open. It wasn't much bigger than a jail cell, but it looked infinitely more comfortable, with carpeting, an inviting bed, and low lighting. There weren't any windows, but a video screen inset in the wall showed an image of a tropical beach, waves lapping the white sand.

"This looks comfortable," he said.

"There's a washroom across the hall," Blanchard told him, and flashing the briefest smile, he said, "Good night."

After Mason washed up, he got undressed, throwing his pants over the back of the lone chair. His phone slipped out, and when he picked it up, it felt hot. He turned on the screen and was informed there was no service. That wasn't surprising. He powered it completely off and dropped it back in his pants.

There weren't any wall switches to douse the lights, and he didn't want to sleep in the electronic glow of a Tahitian beach. He looked around for a remote control, under the pillow and the chair cushions, but there just wasn't one. He considered getting dressed again and going out to look for someone to help, but then he remembered the talking door.

"Turn the screen off," he said, and the image of the beach went black. He climbed into bed, appreciating how comfortable it was, and said, "Lights off too." The room obediently went dark. It was great tech, he thought, and wondered how advanced it was—how far was he from his own time? It had to be at least a decade, he decided, maybe more. He thought through the events of the day, and about going home. Maybe they could send him back to right after he left, and completely avoid the trouble of abandoning Peggy. He'd have to ask Annette.

Drifting into sleep, he had vivid dreams that came and went. He wasn't able to come to awareness or take charge of them. Maybe it was induced by eating all that pastry right before bed, but he dreamed he was dancing with a woman, uncomfortably close, her cloying perfume making him wheeze. He tried to keep his feet moving the right way, but he kept stumbling, twisting his date's waist or arm, completely inelegant and out of time.

FIVE

"Good morning, Mason," a voice said. "You have a visitor."

"What?" he asked, waking in complete darkness. It took him a minute to remember where he was, and that he was a talking to a computer.

"A visitor," it repeated. "Shall I turn on the room lights?"

"Yes," he said, and sat up, rubbing sleep out of his eyes. The lights came up slowly. "What time is it?"

"Just after eight."

Did he really need to be up at this hour? They could have let him sleep a little longer. "So who's here?"

"The director will arrive in seven minutes."

"Great," he said, and stumbled into his clothes, hustling across the hall to splash water on his face. No one was in sight when he stepped back into his room, but a minute later there was a soft knock at the door. He opened it to find Annette, wearing a plain blouse and dark trousers instead of a lab coat. She was younger than he'd thought, seeing her up close like this, her dark hair pulled back from her face.

"Can I take you to breakfast?" she asked.

"Sure." He stifled a yawn and stepped out into the hall. As they walked, he surreptitiously stretched one arm and shoulder back, then the other, trying to wake his body without looking too strange. They seemed to be headed back toward the cafeteria.

"So you're the director?"

"Call me Annette," she said, catching his eye. "I should apologize for the panic that overwhelmed us when you arrived."

"I shouldn't have stepped through."

"I understand. People in your time had trouble reining in their emotions," she said.

He looked at her askance. People here weren't much different, he thought, in light of how she and Blanchard had been hectoring each other last night. Louie was the only one who had seemed even remotely emotionally stable.

"We're calling it an industrial accident," she continued. "The whole project is a learning process. Every part of it involves technical innovations, so unexpected things are bound to happen."

They passed a young woman in the hall, who smiled and greeted Annette in the bright-eyed, respectful way that only a subordinate would. When they entered the cafeteria, it was a lot more crowded than the night before, and several people greeted her with consistent deference and admiration—she was clearly a lot of people's boss. They filled their trays from the food cases, Annette taking half a bagel, and Mason happy to find a lot of fruit. He got himself a double espresso from the machine and followed her to a table near the window, spending a moment admiring the dewy lawn and the hillside still streaked with morning mist.

"So you built a time-travel machine," he said to her once she'd settled into her chair.

"I like the way you phrased it last night," she said. "A 'temporal hole-punch.'"

"You people must spend a lot of time comparing notes. I said that to Louie, or maybe Blanchard, not to you."

"Blanchard," she said, smearing jam on her bagel and looking up at him briefly. "And it's classified."

"But I already know what's going on. Besides, who am I going to tell?"

"Regardless, I can't talk about it," she said quietly, furrowing her brow. "This is just breakfast, Mason, not a meeting."

He took a long sip of his espresso. "Does 'director' mean you're the boss of this whole place?"

"I am the ranking physicist, yes, but I only supervise Blanchard and Qualtrough directly."

"Who's Qualtrough?" he asked, remembering there had been a third person at the controls when he'd first glimpsed this place.

Emotion flashed in Annette's eyes, but she quickly

regained her composure. "He's gone," she said firmly, looking away and taking a bite of her bagel.

"Blanchard mentioned that name, back in your lab." He tried to remember what exactly had been said.

"It's a shame he'll miss the festival," she said. "He has an important role."

"A festival? Is it some science thing?" Mason asked. "Connected to this ... campus, or whatever it is?"

"It's the town festival," she said, nodding toward the window. "The town is right there, across the Green. And this is a research facility. It's called the Sarté Institute."

"So there's a town. I find that reassuring."

"It's where our support staff live, but it's a sleepy little place. The festival is the most excitement there is all year."

Mason swallowed a mouthful of blueberries. "Annette, when can I leave? You said it would be eighteen hours. Is that soon?"

"Eighteen hours is an approximation. The machine has to be recalibrated and primed. That's proceeding normally today, but you'll have to bear with us."

"Will you be able to put me back at the moment I left? That would be optimal, I think."

"That's our intention—to aim within a few hours of that."

Mason smiled. It was a relief, and he instantly felt lighter.

"It's difficult to be precise," she continued, "and

we have to keep six hours of separation between connections."

"It must be extremely imprecise," Mason said, "because there certainly wasn't six hours between them. I saw your portal open twice in the space of ten minutes. The first time, Qualtrough was with you."

"Really?" she said, surprised.

"I assume it was him. There were three of you at the control panel, you and Blanchard and a dark-haired guy."

She didn't reply, finishing the last of her bagel, lost in thought.

It wasn't a reassuring reaction. Perhaps her machine didn't work quite the way she thought it did.

Annette looked back at him, as if suddenly remembering something. "I've asked Blanchard to do an interview with you for our records before you go home."

"Of course," he said. "I'm an industrial accident, after all."

She looked away from him and said, "Mr. Blanchard, we're ready for you."

Louie had done that too, Mason remembered. Looking away must be a social cue that the conversation was with someone else. He still couldn't see a cell phone or an earpiece, though. And how had she initiated the call?

"Thanks for breakfast. I'll be in touch," she said, flashing him a smile as she rose from the table.

"I'll be here," he said as she left. He got another double espresso and was about to sit down again when Blanchard appeared.

"Do you want to grab a coffee?" Mason asked him.

"Actually, we'll go upstairs. Bring that with you, if you like."

He slammed the espresso instead, leaving the empty cup on the table, and followed Blanchard back into the corridor. He led him up a different set of stairs than the ones he'd come down with Annette, and eventually stopped at a door, pushing it open for Mason to step inside. It was a small meeting room, not much bigger than where he'd slept, with a conference table and six chairs.

Blanchard sat at one side and said, "Sit wherever you like."

Mason took a chair at the end of the table, adjacent rather than across from him, to give the impression, he hoped, that he was cooperating. He glanced around the room. Even though there were no visible signs of surveillance, he was certain the conversation would be recorded. If they had invisible phones, surely they had invisible cameras.

"We'd like to get some background about you," Blanchard began, "and how the incident occurred."

Mason looked to at the ceiling, rather than at Blanchard, and in a loud voice said, "I understand." He wanted Blanchard to know that he knew they were being surveilled, but Blanchard just looked mystified.

"You said earlier you work as a psychic. Do you have a storefront? Does it involve palm reading and communicating with the dead?"

Mason snorted. "Neither. I do research. Missing people, robberies, that kind of thing."

"How do your clients find you?"

"Online, and by word of mouth."

Blanchard nodded, but didn't speak, looking at the wall. Mason could hear a faint whisper, just above the silence. Was someone feeding him questions?

Rather than waiting for him, Mason asked, "Why was Annette so upset that Qualtrough left? Did they have a fight or something?"

Blanchard looked surprised. "What do you know about Qualtrough?"

"I saw him through your portal, and you said something about him to Annette, like 'Qualtrough left because you're so hard on us.'"

He stared at Mason for a few seconds, surprise shifting to curiosity. But he continued with the interview. "You spoke about psychic time slips," he said. "We're trying to figure that out. Nothing was ever published on the matter—our work is the first. So you're lying about that, are you not?"

"Nothing was published in your world because psychics aren't scientists. But it's as real as what your machine does."

Blanchard suppressed a smile. "I doubt that."

Mason felt his ears burning. It doesn't really matter what this guy thinks, he reminded himself. "Whatever floats your boat," he said.

"Why were you in the abandoned building the night you stepped through?"

"It's not abandoned. There were tenants, and they

75

kept hearing your portal opening up. They thought it was the ghost of a woman who died in the building. I was there to investigate."

He frowned. "We researched the matter carefully. We know it was an empty building, red-tagged in the 1994 earthquake."

Mason shook his head. "You're wrong. It's a functioning commercial space. A bit run-down, but still in use." He thought about it for a second. "That earthquake wasn't anywhere near there. And if it had been red-tagged, it would have been repaired or torn down soon after."

Blanchard listened to the whispering voice again for a minute, his gaze fixed on the tabletop. It was annoying, knowing there was another party to the conversation. But at least Mason had figured that out. Otherwise Blanchard's behavior would have been completely disconcerting.

"Why did you step through the portal?"

"It was a flash of anger," Mason said. Raising his voice and looking up at the ceiling again, he added, "Which I now very deeply regret." And to Blanchard, "You called me an orangutan, Blanche, and I wanted to confront my bully."

He scowled. "Don't call me Blanche. And I'm not a bully."

"Keep telling yourself that," Mason said, and folded his arms.

Blanchard listened again, then looked back to Mason. "Were you involved in rioting or interpersonal violence in your time?"

"What?" he said, angry now. "No."

Blanchard held up his hands, as if to say, "Relax," then looked away, listening.

"Listen to me," Mason said loudly, "not your handlers. If they have questions for me, tell them to come in here and look me in the eye. Is it Annette?"

"It's not a person," Blanchard said, confused.

"I have questions for both of you. Was Qualtrough her boyfriend, or was he yours? You both get squirrely at the very mention of his name."

Blanchard cocked his head to one side. "How did you know I'm gay?"

"I'm not sure. I guess I have good gaydar. I'm right, though—you two were together."

"It's so interesting that someone from a bygone era can discern that," he said, his eyes bright, finally engaging with Mason.

"Well, we have to stick together. At least we did in my day." He wanted to ask, "How bygone is bygone?"—that word made it sound so far away—but he didn't.

"I love that idea. Camaraderie that transcends sex and romance."

Mason nodded, grateful that the debriefing had been derailed. "So what happened to Qualtrough?"

Blanchard hesitated. He wanted to talk about it, make the connection, Mason could tell. Finally he glanced up at the wall and said, "Interview complete."

Mason grinned.

"You're right," Blanchard said, leaning forward.

"He was my boyfriend. We had a fight." He raised his eyebrows. "Not your kind of fight," he said, holding up a palm. "Just a verbal altercation."

"I knew what you meant," Mason said pointedly.

"Anyway, he was stressed out, I think, and not handling it very well. Two weeks ago, he stepped through the sphere, just like you did."

"You're kidding me," he said. "So this industrial accident thing has happened before. Where did he go?"

"Los Angeles. I presume he's still wandering around there."

"Does Annette know that?"

"She was there when he left," he said. "She knows exactly what's going on."

"That explains why she was worried about him too."

"We think he planned it at least a few hours ahead, because he took some of the historic cash from the staging lab. And he put on a vintage suit." He looked sad at the memory.

"Why would you have those things lying around? Are you planning to send people through the portal?"

"Why else would we build it?" he said. "But that's years away. We have to perfect the technology first."

"And figure out where you're pointing that thing," Mason added, raising his voice and looking up at the ceiling. "Maybe try to find an actually empty building."

"We were both so happy when you came through."

"Really? You seemed completely freaked out. You

basically had me arrested."

"We had to do that," Blanchard said, leaning back in his chair. "What would you do if you saw a Viking berserker or a medieval peasant step out of the past? You'd have them risk-assessed, at the very least."

"Or even a twenty-first-century orangutan," Mason said, raising his eyebrows.

"Exactly. We were happy because you made it through unscathed. That means Qualtrough probably survived it too."

"You must be worried about him."

"Terribly worried. He must feel so lost."

"When I go back," Mason said, "maybe I can track him down. Missing persons is kind of my job. I could bring him back to the portal."

"Mason, you don't understand. He went to the other target—in the 1950s."

"Seriously?" Mason asked, appalled. "Why would he do that? It was a terrible time for us, and for people generally."

"I can't answer that. I think he was irrational, and he did it in a fit of pique. And now," he said, his eyes growing moist, "it might be irreversible."

"Have you looked for him?"

"We're doing everything we can do. We've opened the portal several times, hoping that he'll be there and come back. It's not safe to aim too close to a previous link on that end, and resetting the machine means we can only try every few days. We've opened the sphere for him six times so far."

"But he's never there."

Blanchard looked at the table, lips pressed tight, blinking to keep it together.

"Why don't you let me go after him?"

"It's not safe," he said, looking up.

"I've already done it, man. Think about it."

Blanchard watched him for a minute, calculating. "Your era is a lot closer to then than we are."

"OK, that's alarming."

Blanchard waved his hand dismissively. "Still, I can't imagine Annette letting that happen. It was very nice of you to offer."

"Don't just reject the idea," Mason insisted. "I've done this—I slipped back decades once. It was just for a day, but I was really there."

He sighed. "I don't want to call you delusional to your face, but that's impossible. There's no such thing as psychic time-slips, or psychic power."

Mason thought for a minute, watching him. "I can demonstrate it."

Blanchard grinned. "How?"

"Give me your ring."

"Why?" he asked, suspicious.

"Just hand it over," Mason said, waggling his fingers. "I'm going to read it."

Blanchard pulled it off his finger and slid it across the table.

"Nice," Mason said, leaning forward to examine it without touching it. It was a simple undecorated band, untarnished and unmistakably gold. "How long have you had it?"

"A couple of years. Qualtrough gave it to me."

"So you two were serious."

"Are you reading it now?"

Mason grinned. "I have to touch it. It's called psychometry. I can pick up residual information in the metal."

"OK," Blanchard said dubiously.

"It takes a minute to get into the right frame of mind. If I could ask for silence."

"Sure," Blanchard said, and folded his arms.

Mason closed his eyes, breathing deeply and clearing his mind. Once he had suppressed the random thoughts that popped up, he picked up the ring and pressed it between his palms. He waited for some insight, and gradually a strong image formed.

"Got it," he said, opening his eyes. He handed the ring back to Blanchard.

"What did you get?" Blanchard asked, slipping it back on.

"Do you know the infinity symbol from math?" He drew it in the air with his finger, a sideways figure eight.

"As a physicist, I'm quite familiar with it," Blanchard said.

"Well, I saw it floating on a field of dark blue— really dark, like midnight blue."

Blanchard's expression changed. "Really?"

"Does it mean anything to you?"

"Qualtrough and I drank a brand of bourbon with that symbol on the label. It was one of our rituals, every day after work."

"Yes! And dark blue must mean after sunset, when

the sky turns dark blue," Mason said. "See? It works."

"Actually, the label on the bottle depicts the symbol on a field of midnight blue. That's why I recognized it."

"Even better," Mason said.

"How did you do that?"

"Psychic power, baby. It's as real as you are."

Blanchard raised his eyebrows. "It goes against everything I've ever been taught. But the chances of you pulling that out at random are infinitesimal."

"Free your mind, Blanchard. Physics doesn't have all the answers. One day there's nine planets, and then they decide there's eight, and suddenly there's nine again. So which is it?"

Blanchard smiled. "That's not physics."

"Close enough," Mason said.

"I think I'm going to reserve judgment for now."

"That's a step forward, at least. So will you pitch the idea to Annette? I know LA, and I know what life was like in that era. I'd love to try to find your boyfriend."

"I'm headed to the lab. I'll mention it."

"Great."

"Right now the problem is, I really shouldn't leave you alone."

"You left me alone overnight. I'll hang out in the café, or out on the lawn. Can I go outside? It's not radioactive, is it? I never saw anyone out there. Do I need a space suit?"

Blanchard laughed. "It's completely safe—and unpolluted."

"So let me go. What am I going to do, steal something? I have a feeling your magic doors would stop me if I did."

He looked at Mason, considering the idea.

"Dude, I'll behave. I'm not a berserker, and you're my only ticket home."

That seemed to convince Blanchard. He rose to leave and said, "I'll find you when I have updates. Enjoy the day."

Mason followed him out of the room, but Blanchard went off in the direction opposite from the way they'd come. Mason walked the other way. It felt good to be on his own.

He thought he could find his way back to the cafeteria, but he quickly realized there was no signage anywhere, not even room numbers. He wandered around for a few minutes before realizing he was completely lost. Standing in a corridor that looked just like all the others, he muttered, "Where's the damn cafeteria?"

"Do you see the restroom, on the left?" a voice said, as clearly and as close as if he were listening through a set of good headphones. It was the software voice that had woken him this morning.

"Actually, no," he said, looking up at the ceiling, but not seeing the source of the sound.

"It's the second door ahead. The double door just past that is a stairwell. Take the stairs down and make a right."

"Thank you," he said, and pushed through the doors into the stairs. It was remarkable tech, and somehow it knew where he was—when he made the turn at the foot of the stairs, it spoke again, keeping pace with him and speaking directly into his ears.

"Turn at the next open corridor, then go right. The cafeteria is just a little farther."

Through the cafeteria windows, the sun was blazing on the gloriously green grass outside. He had to go out and enjoy it, clear his head, even if just for an hour. He looked in the food cases for something to take with him, but he needed a way to carry it.

There never seemed to be anyone working behind the cases. He spotted a guy in overalls back there, squatting under the counter next to an access panel that he'd pulled off, a toolbox open beside him.

"Do you know where I could find a bag?" Mason asked him, leaning over the counter.

The guy looked up, startled. "I don't work here."

"All evidence to the contrary," Mason said, glancing at his toolbox. "You dress like that on your day off? I just need something to carry some fruit in."

His eyebrows shot up, and he hesitated, but then got to his feet and walked through a doorway, returning a minute later with a mesh bag in hand, wordlessly handing it to Mason.

"Perfect," he said. "Thanks, man."

The guy didn't reply, but watched Mason walk back to the food cases.

It was getting uncomfortable, Mason thought, seeing the guy in his peripheral vision standing there gawking at him, but eventually he squatted down at his work site again.

The bag had string handles, and once he'd loaded it with apples and pears and grapes, he found he could sling it over one shoulder and under the other arm so the fruit hung on his back—a makeshift backpack. He was adjusting it for comfort when he saw Louie across the room. He wondered if it was just chance to see him here, but he eyeballed Mason and walked directly toward him. Blanchard must have told him that he wanted to go outside.

"Going for a walk?" Louie asked cheerfully, putting his hands on his hips.

"Hey, man. Yes, that's the plan. Where should I go?"

Louie looked out the windows and said, "Well, the town is across the Green, on the left, but that's boring. On the other side of the Green you'll see a trail leading up into the mountains. We call them mountains," he said, leaning closer, as if it was confidential information, "but they're really just hills compared to the ones you have in California. You can walk for hours, and there won't be many other people, even though it's a beautiful day."

"Sold. Mountains it is," Mason said.

Louie reached into his pocket and handed Mason a little metal disk, about the size of a poker chip. "Take this with you."

"What is it?" he asked, flipping it over. It was blank except for a lengthy string of numbers and letters printed across the middle.

"A tracking device," he said simply. "If you get lost, I'll come and find you."

"That seems intrusive."

"It's a safety issue, Mason. Everyone else has a chip or a phone."

He had a phone too, but it was powered off, and he knew it didn't work here.

"If you're worried about me getting into trouble, I won't. I know this place is my way home. I'll come back."

"I'm glad," Louie said. "I'm assuming you'd rather have a quiet day in the mountains than go into town to try to start a street gang."

"Why does everyone here assume I'm a gang-banger?" Mason demanded, feeling the color rise to his face.

Louie didn't reply, but cocked his head as if to say, "Aren't you?"

"Unless hiking has changed dramatically, I won't get lost. I'll be back by nightfall." He turned on his heel and walked toward the windows, and then stopped. He turned back. "Where's the way out?"

Louie chuckled and pointed to the corner of the room. It was indeed a door, Mason saw when he walked up to it, even though it was designed to look like the rest of the windows. He pushed out into the sunshine and was immediately overwhelmed by the warmth, and humidity, and the smell of the trees. He considered tossing the tracker into the grass, but slipped it into his pocket instead. It didn't matter if Louie knew where he was all day, and it was probably smarter to do as he asked.

As promised, a trail led into the trees from the

lawn, and he followed it up onto the mountain. He had a view of the Green for a few minutes as the trail ascended, and soon the town came into view. It looked like a typical New England village, white-clad houses clustered around a soaring church spire, a highway passing nearby. He looked back toward the institute, its broad roof covered with shiny black tiles. He couldn't see the end of it; it seemed to stretch on for acres.

Soon Mason was surrounded by forest. He could feel his whole body relaxing, recharging from being immersed in nature. The East was so much lusher than his part of the world, the plant life so much more exuberant, a treat for the senses. He walked fast enough to work up a sweat, and stopped when he came to a little stream, perching on a rock on the bank to eat his fruit, lulled by the movement of the water. Louie had been right: there was no one else on the trail.

Things worked differently here, he thought, mulling over breakfast with Annette and his interview with Blanchard. Louie was calm, as was the guy in the cafeteria, to the point of being passive. But they didn't have an objective understanding of themselves, if Annette thought they were less emotional than Mason was. The fortress of scientific arrogance was delusional, but that was the status quo in Mason's era too.

He liked the idea of going after Qualtrough, but he wondered if volunteering to do it was capricious, possibly foolhardy. As long as the technology worked well enough to get him there and back, and then home to Ned, it wasn't, he decided, gnawing on a pear. The adventure would far outweigh any nervousness he felt about the shortcomings of the machine. When would he have another opportunity to wander around in the distant past?

He felt blissful and calm by the time he returned to the Green, walking down the hillside toward the tall windows of the cafeteria. He had no idea what time it was, but the sun was low in the sky beyond the institute. He walked into the cafeteria and immediately heard the voice of the computer in his ears. It was jarring after the tranquility of the woods.

"Welcome back," it said.

"OK," he said suspiciously. "What do you want?"

"The director would like to meet with you. Would you like to dine with her?"

"Sure."

"One moment." There was a pause, and Mason stood awkwardly between the tables, waiting. Finally it spoke again. "She'll meet you here in forty minutes."

"That works."

He walked toward the corridor and into the warren of the institute, looking for the staircase up to his room. He wanted to wash up, and he'd seen shower stalls in the washroom across from where he'd slept. He couldn't find the stairs, at least not ones that looked familiar. He looked at the ceiling and said, "Where's the room I slept in?"

The software spoke again, directing him up the correct staircase, guiding him through the turns. He looked over his shoulder to make sure he wasn't being observed, and then sniffed his armpit.

"Is there somewhere I can do laundry?" he asked the ceiling.

"I can have some fresh clothing sent to your room. Would that work?"

"I guess," he said.

"Leave your soiled garments outside the shower."

He went into the washroom and stripped down, happy to find a bathrobe hanging in the shower's anteroom. It was a comfortable little space, lined with frosted glass. He piled his clothes on the redwood bench and spent a few minutes under the showerhead, enjoying the feeling of the hot water on his scalp.

He put on the bathrobe when he was finished but scooped up his clothes and sneakers. He wasn't convinced the replacements would be there yet, or that they'd fit, and he didn't want to be left without any. But they were there, waiting for him, neatly folded on the chair beside the bed. They were the same style as what he was wearing, except in lighter colors, tan chinos and a charcoal-gray polo shirt, and they fit surprisingly well—possibly better than his own. After emptying his pockets and stuffing his keys and phone into the new pants, he took his dirty clothes back across the hall and left them outside the shower, as the computer had instructed.

He stretched out on the bed, just for a minute, wary of falling asleep.

"Can you tell me when it's time to go meet Annette?" he asked.

"I'll wake you in eleven minutes."

"I'm not going to sleep," Mason said, but as soon as he closed his eyes he drifted off, starting awake when the voice summoned him.

"It's time to leave for your dinner, Mason."

"Thanks. And thanks for the clothes, by the way. I feel like a new man."

"You're welcome."

"I think you'll have to direct me to the cafeteria again."

"Of course," it said, and spoke in his ear at various points along the way. It was uncanny how clear and omnipresent it was, and eventually he stopped looking at the ceiling when he talked to it.

He arrived in the cafeteria at the same time as Annette, and she greeted him warmly as they went to the food cases together. She was wearing a cardigan over her blouse now, despite the heat of the day outside. Mason loaded a plate with grilled cauliflower and string beans and red peppers.

"What do you think the soup is?" he asked Annette, swirling the ladle in the tureen and examining the contents. But she was chatting with another deferential underling, enthusiastic for the chance to make small talk with the boss.

The software voice answered. "Split pea and carrot."

"Is it vegan?"

"Yes."

He poured a bowl of it and found utensils, then went to sit with Annette.

"How was your walk?" she asked, smiling and meeting his eye.

She seemed genuinely interested. He didn't even bother asking her who had told her that he'd been outside—they all seemed to know everything he did and said. Either they were all extremely gossipy, or everything was being recorded and summarized.

"I loved it—you live in a beautiful part of the world," he said, cutting into his cauliflower. "How's the recharging going?"

"There have been some delays," she said, focusing on her plate and not meeting his eye, "which isn't unusual. These are complex systems and intricate procedures. We should be back online sometime late tomorrow."

"As long as it's going to happen," Mason said, scanning her face, but he didn't detect deception. This place was intriguing, but he was starting to feel homesick, and he didn't even want to consider the possibility that he might not be able to get home. "You know, I realized today that there are no signs anywhere. None of the offices are labeled, none of the food in the cases."

"You've used the voice guidance, haven't you?"

"I figured it out. But have you given up literacy for that?"

She looked up from cutting her string beans. "People can still read. It's just less necessary than in pretechnological times."

"OK," Mason said dubiously.

"By the way, I appreciate your offer to go after

91

Qualtrough," she said. "It's very generous. But I'm afraid we can't do that."

"Why not? I've already been through the portal, and I'm intact. I can do it again."

She shook her head. "It's against all our protocols."

"Fine," he said flatly. He drank some soup and watched her for a minute. "I know you think I'm this whole delusional berserker-orangutan-gangster man," he said, swirling his index finger in the air, miming a tornado. "But I do this for a living. If you want Qualtrough back, I'm your guy."

She looked at him thoughtfully but didn't reply.

There wasn't anything more he could say to make his case, short of haranguing her. "So who runs this place?" he asked. "Government or industry?"

"The funding is from Harold Sarté, the scion of an ice cream empire."

"Gross."

"What's gross about ice cream?" she said, puzzled. "Everyone loves ice cream."

"I'm sure the cows don't love it."

"Sarté ice cream is made with almonds, not cows. You asked Louie about vegan food yesterday too. Is it hard to get vegan food in your era?"

"Yes and no. I guess I'm making assumptions that don't apply here."

"Well, there's a whole cooler full of Sarté over there," she said, gesturing vaguely to the food cases. "You should try it."

"I will," he said. "But I wonder—why does an ice cream scion need a time-travel machine?"

"He didn't ask for it. We do undirected research here. The founder is involved only at a superficial level."

"Of course," Mason said.

He'd heard of this before—it was just a tax dodge, a robber baron using a private foundation to shelter his fortune.

"So what was Qualtrough like?" he asked.

"Well," she said, setting down her fork and sitting back. "That's a good question. He was a bit unstable, and impulsive, like people were in your era. I'd also say carefree. He was a decent person."

"Blanchard seems pretty broken up about it. Why do you think he left like that?"

"I've no idea. Perhaps he thought it would be a lark for a day or two, a way to throw a wrench into the works, thumb his nose at all our careful preparations."

"Why do you think he hasn't come back?"

"Maybe he likes it so much where he went, he doesn't want to come back. Or maybe …"

"You think he didn't make it?" he asked. "A fatal industrial accident?"

She sighed. "You made it through, which is encouraging. All I can do is continue opening the portal and hope that he shows up."

Mason nodded, finishing his vegetables. "You said you'd miss him in the town festival. What was he going to do there?"

"He plays the part of the Hunter," she said. "I need to figure that out tonight—the event is tomorrow."

Eying her, an idea came to him. Festivals were where you could see people shed their everyday veneer, and really understand their culture. Participating in one would be a lot more interesting than sitting around the cafeteria or that windowless bedroom.

"Could I fill in for him? My departure isn't until late, you said. How difficult is it?"

"You'd do that?" A smile spread over her face. "You remind me of him. You'd be perfect."

"If it's not too much work—"

"None at all," she said, more animated now than he'd ever seen her. "It's pure fun. I'll introduce you to the other performers. We'll go into town." She glanced toward the window and said, "What time is it?"

"How would I know?" Mason said.

She held up a finger and stared into space for a few seconds, listening. "We can leave now," she said, looking at Mason again. "Have you eaten enough?"

"Let's go," he said, and followed her out onto the Green. It was cooling off, as the sun was out of view, only the upper reaches of the mountains directly illuminated in the fading orange light. The town gradually appeared as they crossed the field, first the church spire and then the white houses.

"Where are all the cars?" he asked. They walked into the town, and the streets were paved, but nary a vehicle was in sight. It would be a perfect place to ride a bike.

"They're kept outside town until someone needs one."

"So is this festival a big deal?"

"It doesn't attract people from elsewhere, but it's important in that it connects the town with the institute. Maintaining the tradition means maintaining good bridges."

"You sound like a politician," he said.

She grinned. "I guess some of my job is politics." Stopping in the street, she announced, "We're here."

Mason looked up at the storefront. It was a pub, THE PLOUGH inscribed in bold letters above the door. A shingle hung over the street, a colorful painting of a furrowed field with the namesake antique implement parked on it, handles swooping skyward.

Inside, there were a few people at the bar. Annette led him to a table near the front window.

"Is this a full-on English place where we have to order at the counter?" he asked her, but she had already caught the eye of the barkeep.

"Good to see you, director," the woman said, lifting the gate and stepping over to their table, folding her hands behind her back. "Ready for the festivities?"

"As ready as we ever are," she said amicably.

"I've doubled up on pale ale—I ran out of it last year. What can I bring you?"

"A pint of that for me," she said, and looked to Mason.

"The same," he said.

The barkeep nodded curtly and stepped away.

"Are you sure you're not in the military?" Mason asked her. "Everyone treats you like a general."

She laughed. "It's just because I have seniority,

and I know everybody. Like I said, it's good to have bridges."

Before their drinks arrived, Annette stood to greet a man who came through the front door. He was older, with unkempt gray hair and a full beard.

"The Green Man," she said. "This is Mason." And to Mason, "The Green Man has a lot of seniority in the town—he's my counterpart outside the institute."

Mason stood, and the Green Man clapped him on the back. "Sit," he said, and shouted to the barkeep, "a tankard of pale ale," before sitting down with them.

He seemed more real than anyone Mason had met here, carrying a few extra pounds, wearing bold black-and-red plaid, and grinning broadly before they'd even met.

"Do you have another name?" Mason asked.

"It's Carl. But it's festival time—call me the Green Man."

The barkeep set down their beer glasses, and Annette said, "Cheers."

"Thanks for volunteering to participate," the Green Man said to Mason, wiping beer foam out of his mustache with the back of his hand. "Are you new at the institute?"

"Very new," Annette said quickly, shooting Mason a warning glance. "He's from out of town. Way out of town."

"California," Mason offered. "So what's the festival all about?"

"You'll see it as it unfolds. It's essentially a nature

festival," the Green Man said. He studied Mason for a few seconds. "You're a bit taller than Qualtrough, but I think the tunic will fit you."

"I'm supposed to be the Hunter, right? What will I be doing?"

"It's an important role," he said, leaning back in his chair. "You shoot an arrow at the Fox."

"Really?" Mason said. "There's no way I could kill a fox."

"You're not going to kill anything," Annette said. "The Fox is a character like yours, wearing orange."

"The hunter always misses the Fox," the Green Man added. "The Fox always gets away."

"OK," Mason said, perplexed, and took a long sip of his beer.

"You'll have a bow, but the arrow is imaginary," Annette said, and sat back, a satisfied look on her face, as if she'd just clarified everything.

"It sounds like I can handle it. I might need a bit of coaching."

"I can show you," the Green Man said, setting his beer glass aside and pulling a rolled-up sheet of plastic out of his pocket. It looked like the bamboo mat that Ned used to make sushi rolls, but when he flattened it on the tabletop, it lit up like a video screen. The Green Man swiped and poked at it, then slid it toward Mason. It was a striking piece of technology, with no buttons or borders. He was mesmerized, gently feeling the edge of the device with his fingers.

"This is from last year," the Green Man explained, and Mason focused on the image. A group of about a dozen people in costumes were arrayed on the street in front of The Plough, grinning for the camera, some with beer glasses in hand.

"That's the Hunter," Annette said, pointing to a man at one side wearing a brown tunic and pointed cap with a bright red feather in it.

"So that's Qualtrough," Mason said. He touched the screen and tentatively gestured to zoom in on him. He wasn't bad looking, maybe around Blanchard's age, but with lighter skin and short dark hair. He was taller than the others in the photo, and had a strong jaw. He'd fit right in in 1952.

Up close he saw that what he'd assumed was a red feather was really a scalloped oak leaf. He zoomed out and looked at the other characters. The Hunter had an odd costume, but no more so than the rest. The Green Man was at the other side of the group, wearing a long green tunic with leafy vines draped over his shoulders, a wild wreath of green leaves tangled in his hair.

"Who are the other characters?" Mason asked, sipping his beer.

The Green Man counted with his fingers to enumerate them. "The Green Man, the Hunter, the Fox—"

"Which one is the Fox?" Mason asked, and the Green Man pointed to a young woman. Her costume was really just a dark orange vest and trousers with a black turtleneck.

"And the Drummer," he continued, pointing to the one with a marching drum at his waist and a peaked military cap. "It's always a kid."

"A youth," Annette corrected.

"Right," the Green Man agreed. "A teenager. And the last one is the Maiden." In the image, a woman standing next to the Green Man wore a long royal-purple dress and a voluminous wig. It was an odd juxtaposition—her complexion was South Asian, but the fake hair was Nordic platinum blond.

"Who are all the others?" Mason asked. "In white, with the ears?"

"The Hares," Annette said. "I'm going to be one this year. There are six of us."

Their ears didn't look like rabbit ears, mere bumps on top of their heads, but they wore uniform knee-length white tunics, distinguishing them from the other players.

"So, what do we do?" Mason asked.

"We parade through the town for all to see," the Green Man explained. "I lead, followed by the Hares, and then the rest. The Drummer keeps time. There's some eating and drinking. The Fox will tease you, and you can give chase. Have some fun with it, but don't take a shot."

"That part comes after the dance," Annette said.

The Green Man nodded. "We make our way to the Green, where the Hares do a little dance. I'll give you the high sign after that, when it's time for you to shoot."

"So I'll have the bow, and I just pretend to shoot an arrow at the Fox?"

"No," Annette said. "You really shoot. The arrow

is imaginary." She leaned forward and held his gaze. "The difference is subtle, but it's important. You really try to hit the Fox, but you miss. The closer the shot, the better."

The Green Man drained his tankard and said, "You'll do fine. Can you be at the church at eight?"

"I'll be there," Mason said.

"I have to be up much earlier than that, so I'm going to take my leave." He stood and embraced Annette, then ducked out into the night.

"I have to be up early too," she said. "Can you find your way back to the institute? I live in town."

"Of course," he said, and took a last swig from his glass.

"I'll see you in the morning, then," she said. The beer must have lowered her inhibitions, as she gave him a quick little hug before waving to the barkeep and leaving.

He had to smile. It was a sea change from her first reaction to him, just yesterday. He nodded good night to the barkeep and went out to the street. It was odd that they were so trusting of him, letting him wander around alone late in the evening. But the software in the building always seemed to know where he was, so perhaps he was being monitored more than he knew. He reached into his pocket and felt the poker chip that Louie had given him. He knew it was a tracking device, and he was carrying it around willingly. How could he complain about it when he was complicit in his own surveillance?

Strolling across the Green, he thought of Gilbert,

a friend of Ned's. He was always up for a conspiracy tale—he would love this stuff. "They're watching your every move," he could hear Gilbert saying, wild-eyed and emphatic. And Ned—he felt a twinge of longing at the unplanned separation. If things worked out right, Ned might not even know he'd been gone, but still, it was unbearable to imagine how far away Ned was right now.

He tried to make his way from the cafeteria to his little room on his own, but it was just too difficult, and he asked the computer for directions, which made it effortless. He wasn't sure why he was resisting using the system. Annette had implied that everyone relied on its guidance.

Back in his room, he got undressed and climbed into bed. "Can you wake me at seven?" he asked the air.

"Of course."

"Douse the lights, please."

The festival didn't sound too difficult, although he didn't quite understand it. He thought about the symbolism of the bow and arrow, and the missed shot. It was a pretend arrow, he reminded himself, not a pretend shot. Why was that important? It made it feel like more than acting. He could do it, of course, imagining the arrow was real and missing the Fox. Even though he didn't understand it, logically there must be a good reason to do it that way, and he wanted to live up to it.

Drifting into sleep, he saw geometric shapes, rings and triangles looping and diving through one another, repeating and forming patterns. It wasn't insightful, he decided, not bothering to wake himself up to remember.

SIX

"Good morning, Mason. It's seven o'clock."

Swimming up from the depths of sleep, he soon figured out what was going on. "Lights," he mumbled, and pulled on his clothes before stumbling over to the washroom to clean up. He put his head under the cold-water tap in the sink. The shock of it was almost as effective as a shot of espresso.

After making his way to the cafeteria with the help of the software voice, he sat for a few minutes to drink a coffee and munch on a bowl of berries. The place was quiet. Maybe everyone had the day off for the festival. On the way out he took an apple to eat on the walk across the Green. It was another beautiful day, perfect for an outdoor event.

In the town, there were pedestrians around, some

of whom greeted Mason with a friendly word, but still no cars. Even more unusual, there were no stop signs or traffic lights. He hadn't noticed that last night, only that the place felt different. He'd assumed it was because Vermont was bound to look different from Southern California. But the complete absence of the means of traffic control, now that he saw it, was jarring. Just like within the institute, printed cues seemed to have withered away.

He used the soaring steeple to locate the church, and found the doors to the hall next to it propped open, a small crowd gathered inside. The Hares and the other players were getting dressed, and several people were helping them, pulling the costumes and props out of boxes that were spread around the room.

The Green Man spotted him at the door and waved him over.

"Hey, Carl," he said.

He scowled and said tersely, "You need to chill out, Hunter."

Mason tried again. "Hey, Green Man."

The Green Man's face softened. "Much better." He was already dressed in forest green, leaves and vines wound around his body and through his hair. Even his beard sprouted ivy.

"Don't step into the forest, or you'll disappear," Mason said. "Your foliage looks real."

"I picked it this morning," he said, and turned to the others. "Everyone—it's the Hunter."

Several voices shouted "Huzzah!"

The Green Man proceeded to introduce him to

people, using only their character names. The Fox was a young woman, the same person as in the photo from the previous year that he'd seen last night, and the Drummer was the same teenager, a little taller now, already wearing the drum at his waist and warming up, filling the room with its martial beat. The others just talked over it, busy with their preparations. The Green Man introduced the helpers by their names, which Mason didn't try to remember, but some were unusual. There was a Maria and a Mikey, but also a Nassau and a Burly.

"Where's my cap?" the Drummer demanded, and the one named Burly tossed it to him from across the room.

"This is the Maiden," the Green Man said, presenting a guy half a head taller than Mason. He rarely met people taller than he was, and it felt strange to look up to talk to him.

"Nice to meet you, Hunter," he said. "I'm sure your costume is here somewhere. I haven't got the wig on yet, but the dress still seems to fit." He smoothed the purple fabric over his chest.

"It looks great," Mason said.

"Where's the Hunter?" a woman called from the other side of the room.

"I guess I'd better get dressed," Mason said, excusing himself.

His helper introduced herself as Cam-Cam, and then sized him up. "I think the tunic will fit you," she said. "But if it's too tight, we can do a quick alteration." She started digging through a box of clothes.

"How many Hares are present?" the Green Man yelled. Four people called out "Here," and the Green Man announced, "Two Hares yet to come."

Cam-Cam held the brown tunic against Mason's shoulders. "Do you want to try it?" she said, not sounding convinced it would fit him.

"Sure," Mason said. "With or without the shirt?"

"I'd take it off. You'll overheat."

He pulled it off and slipped the tunic over his head. It smelled musty, but it was much softer than it looked. The armpits were a little snug but not uncomfortable, and the garment was short, ending just below his waist.

"Can you rotate your shoulders?" Cam-Cam asked. He demonstrated a couple of arm rolls, and she said, "It looks OK."

"It's fine," he said.

She handed him the pants. They were knee-length, so at least he'd stay cool.

"Where can I put my clothes?" he asked.

"Hang them on a peg." She nodded to the back of the room, and he saw that one wall was already adorned with a row of the other characters' street clothes.

As he was taking off his pants he saw Annette come in, accompanied by an unfamiliar man.

"Hares five and six have arrived," the Green Man announced, and many people in the room shouted "Huzzah!"

Mason pulled on the brown shorts and tightened the belt. They were roomy enough to pull up under the hem of the tunic, and the legs were still long enough to cover his knees.

"I am so glad they cover my belly," he said, and Cam-Cam laughed.

"Your hat," she said, handing it to him. It was slightly pointed and had an upturned brim, in the same earthy shade as the tunic and the pants. There were actually two bright-red oak leaves, one pinned on either side, which struck him as unusual; men's hats usually had just one decoration, on the left. But it was a costume, after all, and maybe the point was that he'd be flashing the accent color to everyone, on both sides. He put it on and adjusted the fit. It felt weird to have it on his head, but it was snug enough that it wouldn't fall off.

"Perfect," Cam-Cam said as she appraised his look. "The leaves match your hair."

"What about my sneakers—do these work, or are there other shoes?"

"Keep those antiques," she said. "You'll need them. There's going to be a lot of running around. What about your eyes?"

"What about them?"

"Do you want me to find some eyeliner? It would really make them pop."

"I don't usually wear makeup," he said. "What if I get sweaty and it runs down my face? I'll look like a raccoon."

"I guess it'll be fine," she said, squinting and stepping back to get a different view. "You're just so fair."

He doubted that he was so pasty that people wouldn't be able to tell where his eyes were, but he let it go. It was a performance, after all, and she just wanted him to look the part. But eyeliner seemed like a recipe for disaster—grooming and fashion that involved any degree of precision or finesse usually ended badly for Mason.

"What about the bow?" he asked.

"Oh," she said, raising her eyebrows. "We wouldn't want to forget that." She dug through the box where the costume had been, and then started into another, eventually pulling out the bow and presenting it to him.

Made of wood and shorter than any real bow Mason had seen, it was a prop, without a string and not meant to be strung. But it had a graceful, classic curve to it, and it was old, varnished by the touch of many hands.

"You're ready," Cam-Cam told him. "See you out there."

He thanked her and wandered over to greet Annette where the Hares were getting dressed. She already had her long white tunic on, belted at the waist.

"The Hunter," she said, giving him the once-over. "You really look the part."

"I love the energy in here," he said. "Everyone's so excited."

"Wait till we get out on the street," she said. One of the helpers brought her ears. They were made of wood, or maybe papier-mâché, and they looked old, painted white with a small black mark right at the tip. They were attached to a ribbon that the dresser carefully looped through Annette's hair, fastening it gently behind her neck so that the ears were perched at the front, almost on her forehead.

"Is that all there is to your costume?" he asked.

"The costume is the simple part. I had to learn how to dance—I've been practicing for weeks."

Mason grinned. "I'll look forward to that."

Looking around the room, it seemed that everyone was almost ready. The Hares all had their ears on, and the Maiden had donned the blond wig.

"So why is the Maiden a guy?" he asked Annette.

She frowned. "Why wouldn't it be?"

"Well, the word *maiden* kind of implies a female."

"It's just a character, Mason. Anyone can play it."

The Fox came over to them, in costume now, wearing her rust-colored Capri pants and vest. Her sneakers were bright red, and thick black whiskers had been drawn on her cheeks.

"Hey, Hunter man," she said, loud and aggressive. "I am going to make you run." She mock-lunged at him, stopping short, throwing her arms out as if to bear-hug him.

Annette laughed.

"That sounds like smack talk," Mason said.

"I don't know that word," she said, "but if it means that you're never, ever going to catch me, then yeah, smack it is."

"All right," Mason said firmly, meeting her eye. "It's on."

"Woo-hoo," she bellowed, pumping a fist in the air and dancing away.

The energy in the room was ramping up, the Drummer increasing the tempo, the beat getting more insistent.

The Green Man went to the doorway and raised his arms for quiet.

"It's time," he said. "Dressers, thank you for your help. We'll see you on the Green. Players, let's go."

Everyone clapped, and the Hares assembled at the door with the Green Man. The Maiden waved Mason over to where he was standing, behind the Hares.

"We're after them," he said, "and the Drummer follows us."

The boy came up behind them, playing now with a slower beat, probably so he wouldn't tire himself out, but it was loud, and it already felt relentless. He had donned his cap, and Mason saw that embroidered in gold on the front of the navy-blue fabric was a stylized ship's anchor.

They set off, the ragtag group led by the Green Man, marching purposefully in the middle of the street. The Hares kept together, mostly as a group, sometimes marching in step but usually just walking and chatting, waving to the townspeople who came out into their front yards to wave happily and watch the spectacle. Mason and the Maiden followed the Hares, with the Drummer not far behind. The Fox ran around wildly, sometimes running ahead of the Green Man, sometimes behind the Drummer, stopping often to talk to bystanders. The Green Man was definitely the leader, but the Fox handled public relations.

People whooped and shouted at them, and Mason waved back. The energy and the excitement felt familiar somehow. He wasn't part of any group activity these days, but the feeling of a team with a purpose, doing something collectively, was uplifting, almost primevally familiar.

Being so tall and with the electric blond hair, the Maiden drew a lot of shout-outs from the crowd. Looking at him now in daylight, Mason saw that he hadn't even bothered to shave. The purple dress was unadorned and unbelted, and he wore it flat-chested, lumbering along in flip-flops. He had done his eyes, or maybe Cam-Cam had, but the overall effect couldn't even be called ratchet drag.

"So you've done this before?" Mason asked him.

"A few times," he said, "although my wife played the Maiden last year. The dress is getting tight for me—I should probably pass it on to a thinner person." He paused momentarily to curtsey to a bystander who had shouted to him from the steps of a diner. "Hunter," the Maiden said, "you should be waving your bow around a little."

"Got it," Mason said, and did so, holding the bow in the middle and hoisting it up in the air above his head, looking to the bystanders. The crowd in front of the diner clapped and whooped. He repeated the gesture whenever he saw someone watching him, and always got a happy response.

"You can call me Mason," he said to the Maiden when they were a little farther along, on a stretch of street with few observers.

"Not today, Hunter," he said, and squeezed him around the shoulders.

They came upon a building with a group of children gathered out front, even though it didn't look like a school. The Fox ran through the Hares, especially energetic for the young audience, and then came up behind Mason and tugged on the hem of his tunic, running away again as Mason whirled around to confront her. The crowd loved it, screaming and oohing at her daring. Mason exaggerated his outrage, brandishing the bow in the air and stamping around angrily. They cheered for him too, shouting warnings as the Fox crept up on him again, which he pretended not to notice.

"What?" he shouted to the children, cupping a hand to his ear as if he couldn't hear them shouting "Behind you!" The Fox deftly pushed his cap onto his forehead, momentarily obscuring his vision. Again he made a great display of outrage, painstakingly readjusting the hat and angrily shaking the bow in the air.

"You're a natural," the Maiden said as they turned onto the next street.

"It's a lot of fun," Mason said. "Cathartic, even. I've never done anything like this." They were on another quiet block, so he asked, "Did you know Qualtrough? He played the Hunter last year."

"Of course. He used to come to The Plough. He was a good guy. Happy-go-lucky sometimes, depressed sometimes. He had the ego, you know?"

"What kind of ego?"

"Alcoholics always have it. They hate themselves, but the world still revolves around them."

"Interesting," Mason said. He wondered if Ned fit that description. He'd quit drinking before Mason had met him, and he was still a regular twelve-stepper. Ned was opinionated, which could be interpreted as egotistical, but then again, most people were. It was a pointless question, he decided, as it was impossible for him to be objective about Ned.

The route led them through streets all over town, and based on the position of the steeple, they had wound around three sides of it by the time they came to the doughnut shop.

"Doughnuts for the players," the Green Man announced, and the Hares cheered and crowded inside, but Mason hung back.

The Drummer, his instrument silent for the first time since leaving the church hall, stuffed his drumsticks in his pants and beckoned him in.

"No, dude, I can't eat them. I'm vegan," Mason explained.

"What planet are you from?" the boy demanded. "Harold Sarté built this town. Everything's vegan."

The Fox chuckled and imitated him. "Dude," she said, as if it were a funny word.

Mason followed them inside and partook with the others, the proprietor handing doughnuts over the counter in a feeding frenzy that lasted a few minutes. The sugar renewed their energy for the parade once they were back out on the street.

A few blocks later they were under the familiar shingle of The Plough.

"Beer for the players," the Green Man shouted.

The Hares reacted even more enthusiastically, crowding inside. Mason stood at the bar, bow in one hand and beer glass in the other, and drank a pint, worried that it might make him groggy. But before long they piled out onto the street again at the bidding of the Green Man, and paraded the short distance to the Green. Most of the townspeople had gathered, it seemed, including many of the faces they had passed on the streets. He saw Cam-Cam and the other dressers, and recognized a few people from the institute. Louie was there, not in uniform but not looking too relaxed either. He watched passively as the players paraded onto the Green.

The crowd surrounded a vague open space on the lawn, and most of the players dispersed as they arrived, wandering around to talk to friends. Annette stood chatting with Louie, hands on her hips, surveying the scene, and the Maiden stood with his arm draped casually around a woman's shoulder. He recognized her as the Maiden in the photo of last year's group. Even the Drummer had taken a break, talking animatedly to a small group of young people. The Fox stayed in character, running around the edge of the crowd, keeping the energy up, and when she came near, Mason occasionally shook his bow in the air.

Finally the Green Man clapped his hands, and

the crowd quieted down. "Where are the Hares?" he shouted.

They dutifully assembled in the center of the circle, forming two rows of three, facing each other, all in white. Two were men, and Annette was one of the four women. The Maiden went over to where the Green Man was positioned, away from the dancers but not among the spectators either, and waved for Mason to come. He jogged around to join them, and the Drummer started up again at a moderate tempo.

The dancing started with the Hares doing synchronized footwork. It wasn't fast or too complex, despite Annette's implication that it had been difficult to learn. One of the Hares stepped back and danced around behind the other line, replacing a woman who danced across, taking his place. Annette seemed to be having a good time with it, smiling broadly as she played her part. The footwork and switching places continued for a few minutes, the only accompaniment the beat of the drum, until finally they bowed to one another with a flourish, then switched places and bowed again, the tips of their wooden ears almost touching as the two lines leaned together. On the third bow, they held the position longer, and the Drummer stopped. The crowd applauded wildly.

"You're up," the Green Man said quietly to Mason.

He sprang into action, looking around for the Fox. She was on the other side of the Hares, who were still standing together. He ran around them, and she darted into the crowd, reappearing a few seconds later, crouching as she stealthily came up on the other side of the Hares. Mason stopped short and pretended to be flummoxed, spinning around and scanning the crowd, shading his eyes with one hand for a better view. The Fox stood back-to-back behind one of Hares, who giggled and pulled out the hem of her tunic to help conceal her from the Hunter. Mason stroked his chin in mock bemusement, then called, "Come out, come out, wherever you are."

The crowd oohed in anticipation, and the Fox made a break, running away from the Hares. Mason planted his feet firmly, one behind the other, and hoisted his bow, but where was the arrow? Of course, it was in his bow hand. It had been there all along. He quickly notched it into the string and drew it back to maximum tension, his elbow high in the air, squinting to take aim. He focused on the Fox's shoulder as she ran, mentally zeroing in, aiming to barely graze the orange fur he knew was there. He released the missile and his draw arm jerked back, fingers splayed. The arrow flew true, streaking just past the Fox's shoulder, ruffling the fur with the wind of its sharp fury but missing, striking the earth beyond with a thud.

The spectators roared, and the Fox began a victory dance around the perimeter of the circle, strutting and pumping her fists.

"A-a-ah!" Mason shouted in consternation, looking to the sky and shaking his fists. He fell to his knees, set down the bow, and slumped forward, covering his face with his hands.

When he thought it had been long enough, and the cheering subsided, he looked up again. The play seemed to be over. Spectators spilled into the circle, congratulating the Fox, who had finally broken character, the Hares dispersing to join their friends and families. He got to his feet and was congratulated by strangers, who told him "Good job" and "So close, Hunter." He thanked them, shaking hands with a few people when they offered.

The Maiden approached him, the shiny blond locks gone to reveal his own short hair, glistening with sweat. "Hunter," he said, putting his palm on Mason's back, "come and eat with me and my wife."

"Sure," he said, and let the Maiden guide him through the crowd. People were hanging out on the grass, some sitting cross-legged to visit with friends, others spreading out blankets.

"This is my wife, Kavia," the Maiden said, stopping at a blanket occupied by the woman Mason had seen him with earlier. The blond wig lay in a messy heap next to a wicker picnic basket. "Our kids are around here somewhere too."

Kavia didn't rise but greeted him warmly, "Welcome, Hunter."

"So what's it like to be married to the Maiden?" Mason asked her as he sat cross-legged on the blanket.

Kavia laughed. "You may have noticed he's outgrowing the dress," she said.

The Maiden set out a bunch of grapes and some crackers from the basket and handed them each a sandwich.

"They're cucumber," Kavia explained as she unwrapped hers.

117

They chatted about the events of the day, Kavia complimenting them both on their roles.

"I heard that you're new at the institute," the Maiden said after they'd eaten. "Where did you go to school?"

"Very new," Mason said, dodging the question. "I just got here." He looked around at the crowd and said, "I really like your town. There's such a nice mix of people." It really was much more diverse than he'd thought Vermont would be, the townspeople running a riotously colorful gamut.

"We're happy here," Kavia said agreeably.

"Thanks for lunch," Mason said, "but I'm not used to sitting on the ground. My butt's falling asleep."

They waved good-bye as Mason stood and walked through the crowd, greeting people who recognized his garb and consoled him on his near miss. He came across Annette, sitting on the lawn with one of the other Hares.

"Sit with us," she said, waving him over.

He dropped onto the grass beside her, facing the other Hare, who introduced himself as Martin.

"Lemonade?" she asked, offering him what looked like a beer bottle, but when he screwed off the cap it did indeed smell of lemon.

"For a second I thought you were actually going to hit the Fox," Martin said. "You did really well, Hunter."

"You were a good sport," Annette agreed, clinking her own bottle against his. "And such a talented archer. That shot was so close."

"Thanks. It was a lot of fun. What an interesting festival," Mason said.

"Martin, can you give us a minute?" Annette asked.

"Of course," Martin said, rising to his feet. "It's time I found another beer anyway."

"I wanted to talk about your return trip," Annette said quietly once Martin was gone. "You can go home directly, if you'd like, or I've decided you can go after Qualtrough, if you really want to try."

"That's great news," Mason said. "I definitely want to. When will I get another chance to see the 1950s?"

Annette chuckled. "Besides you and Qualtrough, I don't know anyone who would choose that."

"What changed your mind?"

"Seeing you out there today. You took to it so naturally, like you were made to be the Hunter."

"Well, it wasn't especially complicated."

"But you adapted to it without being trained. It means you'll do fine going after Qualtrough."

"I'll do my best. No guarantees, though—Los Angeles was a big city even back then."

"Of course. We had talked about an extraction mission even before you offered, and in the meantime we keep opening the portal. We had no idea who to send. We'd narrowed it down to either police or historians—and then you came through. Some people said we should halt the research altogether because of that, two major incidents in short succession. But then how would Qualtrough get back?"

119

"It would help if you'd connected to a building that's actually empty."

She snorted. "In any case, my colleagues agree that you're clearly the best candidate. You've already done it, and you're practically from there."

"Will the machine be ready tonight?"

"In the morning. There's a little more prep work to do."

"I'll be ready," he said.

A bright-eyed staffer from the institute came to sit with them, and after Annette had introduced them, they all chatted for a few minutes about the festival march and the dance. Eventually Mason excused himself and walked around the edge of the sea of blankets and picnics.

Despite the exhaustion that was setting in, he felt buoyed by the idea of going after Qualtrough, and smiled to himself. It was a little intimidating, the expectation that he'd actually find the guy, which he wasn't convinced he'd be able to do. But he'd done it before, he reminded himself, and he was good at it.

He walked back to the church with his bow in hand. Inside the hall he found the Fox and one of the Hares, changing out of their costumes.

"Hey, Hunter," the Fox said. "You're a great shot. It was so close I could feel it."

"Thanks," he said. "You did great out there too. Where do you get the energy?"

She laughed. "I think the feedback from the spectators is part of it."

"You certainly had them pumped up," Mason

said, putting his hands on his hips. "It's a powerful scene, the Hunter shooting at the Fox."

"It's the climax of the whole day. The dancing thing is interesting," she said quietly, glancing at the Hare, "and everybody watches, but they go wild for the archery and the escape."

"Can you tell me what it means?"

"The festival? I'm not sure. Mostly it's just a tradition. Someone said it's about moving beyond nature's cycles. Maybe not killing the fox represents letting go of hunting. For me, I just like the predictability. Knowing it'll happen every year, getting everybody together for a day."

"I can see the value in that. You did it last year, with Qualtrough, right?"

"We did it together several times. He was a good Hunter. Although last year he got soused at The Plough and missed me by a mile. There was no excitement. Not like there was today."

"Do you think he's an alcoholic?"

"Maybe," she said, squatting to tie her shoes. "I don't know him that well. He seems like a nice enough guy. Bright, but a little listless. Are you planning on usurping his role permanently?"

"No—it was just a favor to Annette because I was available."

She stood upright again. "It might not seem like it on the surface, but she's an important part of the festival. She's one of the biggest boosters."

After she left, he changed back into his own clothes, folding the Hunter's uniform and setting it loosely on the boxes it had come out of. He took a final close look at the bow, running his thumb along it, admiring the wood grain, before setting it on the box and heading back to the institute. Back on the Green no one seemed to recognize him as the Hunter without the getup, and he skirted the picnickers unaccosted.

The cafeteria was quiet and empty, although there was still food on display. He looked up to the ceiling and asked the air, "Can I get a notepad and a pen?"

The software voice spoke directly in his ears and guided him back into the labyrinth, leading him to the door to a supply room. He found a yellow pad, flipping through it to make sure it was nothing more bizarre than paper, and was glad to find a pen that wasn't futuristically abstruse either. He took two, just in case, and went back to the cafeteria, pulled himself a double espresso, and got comfortable at a table.

He spent a long time writing it all down—all about the festival, the characters, taking the real shot with the imaginary arrow. He made notes about the Maiden, the Green Man, the tacit prohibition on real names. A few people came in from the festival from time to time, and one even recognized him, calling out, "Hey, Hunter—great shot." Mason waved in acknowledgment. He'd written most of what he wanted to record and was rereading his notes when Louie came in from the Green.

"I almost didn't recognize you at the festival," Mason said when he walked over. "You were very stealthy in your plain clothes."

"I certainly saw you," Louie said. "You have excellent hand-eye coordination."

"Are you hungry?" Mason asked him. "I was thinking about getting some food."

He hesitated for a second but said, "I guess I can join you for a minute."

Mason got a tray and loaded it with some soup and a little container of Sarté ice cream. Louie skipped the tray and took an apple and a banana.

"I heard that you're going after Qualtrough," Louie said when they sat down.

He nodded, breaking crackers into his soup. "Annette seems to have warmed up to the idea. I just hope I can find him."

Louie watched him for a minute. "People were so different in your time. Fearless."

"I wouldn't say that about me personally," Mason said, grinning. "And people here don't seem fearful."

"There's not that much to be afraid of here."

"You must see the dark side of things in your job. Although you are the most relaxed cop I've ever met."

He shrugged. "I knew you weren't dangerous when I met you. Annette and Blanchard didn't know that right away, and you saw how they reacted."

"Lots of histrionics," Mason agreed. "For me, though, I don't see that there's any danger in what I'm doing. The technology clearly works, and where I'm going isn't the Wild West." He started into his ice cream. It was really good; he could understand why it had built an empire. "So is Qualtrough a drinker?"

Louie looked surprised. "I know he drank, but

from what I saw, he wasn't a drunk. It never seemed problematic. Why do you ask?"

"Just curious. It might help me find him if I know where to look."

"I'd go where the guys are," Louie said. "He's pretty boy-crazy."

For the first time he was able to find his way back to his little room without computer navigation. It didn't seem like much of an achievement considering he'd been here for three days. He spoke to the computer anyway.

"Is it possible to get some clean clothes?" he asked as he walked up the stairs.

"Of course," it said. "Leave your soiled garments outside the shower."

Maybe the system had sensors that could detect he was a little ripe, or maybe he was just predictable, but it had guessed right—he was headed to the shower. He threw his notepad and pens on his bed along with the contents of his pockets, and as he turned to leave, stopped short and looked again: the clothes were already there, neatly folded on the chair, the same gray shirt and tan chinos. Either his need for them had been predicted, or things here worked lightning fast—he'd asked for them just a minute ago.

It felt good to shower after all that activity in the warm sunshine, and he returned to the bedroom clean and content. He tore off the notes he'd made and folded them up, first in thirds and then in half, and put them in a pocket of the new pants, along with his phone and his keys. Climbing into bed, he drifted off almost instantly.

"Lights," he mumbled, and embraced unconsciousness.

In the dream world he found himself walking around the Montclair Security Building again, so shabby and dilapidated compared to the institute. He wasn't aware he was dreaming, reacting rather than acting, walking up the stairs to room 203, dreading it but going anyway, propelled by the irresistible need to look inside. When he stepped through the doorway he found Gladys, all in gray, hair in classic pin curls. She didn't see him, but stood there wringing her hands, looking worried.

"I'm right here," he said, waving at her, but she was oblivious, locked in her own monochromatic world.

SEVEN

"Good morning, Mason. It's seven o'clock."

"What?" he mumbled, coming to consciousness as the lights slowly brightened.

"Mr. Blanchard would like to have breakfast with you."

"Now?" he asked, sitting up so that he wouldn't fall asleep again.

"He'll meet you at the cafeteria when you're ready."

Once he'd dressed and washed up, he found his way downstairs unaided. Blanchard was already at a table and waved when he spotted Mason. Mason grabbed a bowl of oatmeal and pulled a double espresso before joining him.

"I truly appreciate what you're doing," Blanchard said as Mason sat down.

There was none of the perfunctory distance he'd maintained in their interview, Mason thought, meeting Blanchard's eye. He was being sincere.

"Annette says you're better qualified than anyone here. She figures you can handle yourself in the 1950s."

"I'm happy to do it," Mason said. "I've been thinking about it. Why not deposit me there just before he arrives? I can nab him and steer him back here on the next connection."

Blanchard pressed his lips together and shook his head. "That can't be done. We've opened the portal several times in succession on that end, both before he went and then hoping he'd come back afterward. We can't overlap them, so the best we can do is slot you in a few days after his arrival."

"How many days?" Mason asked, gulping at his espresso.

"That's the thing. We're not sure. Minimum about forty-eight hours, maximum maybe ninety."

"That level of precision doesn't exactly inspire confidence," he said, meeting his eye. Was he really going to do this? If they couldn't pinpoint the time, he might get stranded in the 1950s, and that would be a nightmare. He wasn't even sure now why he'd volunteered to go—a misplaced desire to get involved, or a twisted sense of adventure. Ned would tell him it was far too risky.

"You're living proof that it's possible," Blanchard said. "The point in time is variable, but everything else seems to be working."

"What's the plan to get me back?"

Blanchard sipped his coffee before answering. "We'll open the portal every day or two here, as often as we can. It'll be every four to eight hours on that side."

"Okay, so you can't pin down the time. Will the portal at least always be in the same place?"

"Yes. We think the target site is in a commercial building like the one you were in. It was chosen because it was unoccupied at the time."

Mason scoffed. "I've heard that one before."

"You have to understand, the records are spotty. But the room has been empty so far."

Mason set down his spoon and pushed his empty bowl away. "Can I go dressed like this? What about cash?"

"We'll get to that this morning. There's actually a whole subsection in Qualtrough's department that's dedicated to those details."

"What's Qualtrough's department?"

"Historical research," Blanchard said, and watched him intently for a minute, wrapping his hands around his cup. Mason could see the muscles tighten as he worked his jaw, wracked with emotion. "Bring him back to me," he said quietly.

"I can't promise that," Mason said gently, knowing now that he had to follow through. "But I'll try."

Walking through the labyrinth of the institute with him after breakfast, Mason realized that Blanchard was almost certainly using the computer navigation. He could occasionally hear an unintelligible whisper emanating from the vicinity of Blanchard's head, like sitting beside someone on the metro whose earbuds were leaking sound.

They walked into a room that looked something like a commercial kitchen, or a laboratory, except there were no sinks or recognizable equipment, just a high table lined with stools, and cabinets along one wall. Annette was there, wearing her lab coat again, with two younger people in similar garb, both of whom eyed Mason with curiosity.

Annette greeted them when they came in. "Thanks again for volunteering to do this. We've prepared some materials for your trip, including clothing. You can't take anything personal with you, anything from here or from your own time, of course."

"Of course," Mason said. "Set me up—I'm ready to roll."

"Good." She smiled. "I'll see you at the portal." Looking to Blanchard, she said, "Can I leave this in your capable hands?" It was an order rather than a request, and she didn't wait for a reply before she left.

"Mason, this is Kitten," Blanchard said, introducing one of the staffers.

He nodded in greeting. She didn't look feline at all, Mason thought, but was solid and stocky.

"And this is Lil Dove," Blanchard said.

"Does the Lil mean 'little'?" Mason asked him. He wasn't little, either, almost as tall as Mason, with luxe black hair like Ned's.

He looked perplexed. "You'd have to ask my mother. It's spelled L-I-L."

"Got it," Mason said.

"These two have been researching your era," Blanchard said. "The end goal of their work is to be able to send explorers who blend in. They're going to help you prepare."

"You've actually been there," Kitten said, studying his face.

"I've been to my era, not the 1950s," Mason said.

"The historical research department works on them concurrently," Blanchard said. "We think of them as similar."

Mason frowned. "Well, I don't."

"You'd be such a great resource," Kitten continued. "I have so many questions."

"Like what?" he asked.

She thought for a moment. "OK—one thing I haven't figured out is why people wore a chain between their front pants pocket and their back pocket." She drew a line on her right hip with her finger.

"A chain?" Mason said, trying to picture it.

"When they're wearing denim pants, there's sometimes a silver chain hanging at the side of the hip. I've spotted it in many images."

"I guess I've seen that," Mason said, not sure that he had.

"So what's it for?"

"Maybe the chain is attached to a wallet."

Kitten nodded, her eyes bright. "I wondered about that. If you tried to pull out someone's wallet, you'd quickly be confronted by its owner."

"That makes sense," Mason said. "It might also just be a fashion thing. I've never heard of anyone actually getting their pocket picked."

"Kitten, we don't have time for this," Blanchard said. "We need to focus on the matter at hand."

"Of course. If you'll have a seat," Kitten said, assuming a more businesslike tone.

Mason climbed on a stool and watched as she opened a cabinet and brought out some white hand towels and a toolbox. When she opened the box he saw that it was a makeup kit, but there were other things in there as well. She pulled out a pair of swim goggles and a handheld device that looked something like a staple gun. She gave him the goggles, which were completely opaque. He looked at her dubiously.

"To protect your eyes while I shave you," she explained.

"With what?" he demanded.

"A shaver, of course," she said, and waggled the stapler.

"Have you done this before?"

"There's no danger. You want to fit in, don't you? If you're walking around with three days' beard, people will assume you're homeless."

He sighed and pulled on the goggles.

"Chin up," she said, and he tilted his head back, folding his arms to keep them out of her way as she got close to him. He barely felt the device on his skin, but soon smelled the distinctive tang of burning hair. "Done," she said after a minute or so, and put a towel in his hand. He pulled off the goggles and felt his cheek. It was as smooth as if there had never been any whiskers there.

"That's the closest shave I've ever had," he said, using the towel to wipe away the ashy residue.

"It should last three or four days." She picked up another unidentifiable tool and stepped behind him. "Next I'm going to fix your hair."

"Is that really necessary?" he asked. "I don't think I'll need a pompadour to fit in."

"It's just a trim," she said, setting to work. "It needs to be a little tidier."

Mason held still, feeling the device buzzing behind his ears. He closed his eyes and submitted to it. She did much more than a trim—he could feel clumps of hair falling away. After she turned the cutter off, she brushed it thoroughly with what felt like a boot brush, and then he felt a comb running through what was left.

"What are you doing now? It feels wet."

"I'm applying pomade."

"It feels like you're drizzling me with olive oil," he said, shuddering as it adhered to his scalp. He looked to Blanchard to intercede, but he was leaning against the table, hands in his pockets, watching them with an amused look on his face. Lil Dove had disappeared. "Does it wash out, at least?"

She laughed. "Eventually. If you need to reapply it, you can ask at a barbershop. They can shave you as well. They're located in retail districts, typically marked by a red-and-blue striped pole near the door."

"I know what a barbershop is," Mason said flatly.

"Right," she said soothingly, working with a brush again, gently sweeping his hair back from his forehead.

"Can I see?" Mason asked.

She found a hand mirror in her kit and passed it to him.

"I look like I stepped out of a vintage magazine ad for canned spaghetti," he said, holding the mirror out to get a look. His hair still had some length on top, but it was much shorter on the sides, and the pomade had darkened it significantly.

"Printed materials are indeed a major element of how we ascertained what was in fashion," she said. "There were a lot of redheads in the advertisements then, even though statistically you're a small portion of the population."

"Color printing was a new technology, and red really jumps off the page," Mason said.

He craned his head to see the back of his new hairstyle in the little mirror. He had to admit it looked like an authentic 1950s cut. He gingerly touched it, and happily the oil didn't transfer to his fingers.

"Clothes," Kitten said, and went to a cabinet, from which she pulled a gray suit on a hanger and a stack of other garments. She set them on the table and arranged them—a white shirt and undershirt, socks, even boxer shorts. A wide necktie bore an olive-green print of hibiscus flowers. A pair of oxfords and a fedora completed the package.

"That's a lot of clothes," Mason said, dismayed.

"You can change in the next room," Kitten said.

Blanchard must have seen the look on his face. "You're doing really well," he said encouragingly, as if to an eight-year-old.

Mason scooped up the clothes, leaving the fedora on the worktable, and went through the doorway Kitten had pointed out, wondering why there was no door. He found a little table and a chair like the one in the room where he'd slept, along with a full-length mirror.

He dumped the retro clothes on the table and stripped off what he was wearing. It felt odd to put on the boxers—he only wore sporty undies because he cycled everywhere. The effect was breezy, like he was still naked, but putting on the pants helped. They were heavy, made of wool or some other natural fiber, but they fit well, despite the high cuffs and the pleats in front. He wasn't going to wear the undershirt, he decided. It was overkill, and he'd sweat too much. The shirt fit perfectly too, like it had been tailored for him. Flipping up the collar, he tied the necktie, but he had to redo it a couple of times to get the length right. He slipped on the jacket and emptied the pockets of his chinos—keys, cash, phone, and the folded-up notes he'd made last night. He couldn't really take any of it with him, especially the money. Stuffing it all back into the pockets of the chinos, he hastily rolled them up. Hopefully they'd be waiting for him when he got back.

But not the phone. He held on to it for a second, feeling the comfort of its familiar shape and texture. Of course it wouldn't work there, and Annette's prohibition had been clear. But something told him to take it anyway. He glanced toward the doorway, and slipped it into the inside pocket of the suit jacket, then sat down to put on the oxfords. It was creepy to be wearing real leather, if that's what they were made of, but he tied the waxy laces anyway and stood up, turning to the mirror.

Even without the hat, it was a remarkable transformation. He grinned at himself. With the wide lapels and muted tie, he looked like he'd stepped out of a film noir thriller. Ned had recently watched a whole film series from the 1940s about a detective named Buster, and Mason and Peggy had both gotten sucked in and watched with him. In this getup he would fit right into that world. He straightened the shoulders of the jacket and tried buttoning it, then unbuttoned it again. The film detective would wear it unbuttoned, he decided. What was the line Buster had used every time he caught the bad guy?

"Stick 'em up, chump," he said, mimicking Buster's flat intonation.

"What does that mean?" Kitten asked. She was standing in the doorway behind him.

"It's from an old movie," he explained, feeling the color rise to his cheeks.

"Shall I show you how to tie the necktie?"

"I don't think that's changed," he said, irritated now. "But you're welcome to inspect it."

She stepped closer and fondled the knot. "Not bad," she said, and nodded.

He scoffed and stepped away.

"Why didn't you put that on?" she asked, eying the undershirt on the table.

"It's too many clothes. It feels like I'm wearing a snowsuit as it is."

She looked concerned. "It's authentic to the era."

"Nobody will ever know. I'll keep my shirt on."

"All right. I guess it won't matter."

She turned to walk back into the work room, and Mason followed her.

"You look good," Blanchard said, raising his eyebrows. "It really works."

"Kitten, this thing fits me so well," Mason said. "How did you know my size?"

"I had the system measure you." She gestured for him to turn around.

"When?" he asked, holding his arms out and doing a slow twirl.

She ignored the question. "I think it looks right. No visible anachronisms."

"Did Qualtrough get a vintage suit too?" he asked.

Her face clouded. "I had nothing to do with that."

"I should know what he's wearing, though. It might help me find him."

"Look in the mirror," she said. "Same outfit."

"Even the tie?" Mason asked, incredulous.

"His is maroon, but it's the same floral pattern."

"That makes no sense."

"We're not running a tailor shop," she said. "We've only recreated one set of garments."

Mason scanned her face, folding his arms. She denied involvement, but she sounded defensive.

"If the clothes fit," Blanchard said, "why do you look like they're hurting you? You're all pinched and hunched."

"I guess I have to get used to them. They fit, but they're heavy." He rolled his shoulders and tried to relax.

"Have you ever walked on a frozen pond, or a skating rink?" Kitten asked, putting her hands on her hips.

"Probably," Mason said. "Why?"

"Well, it's like that. If you try to minimize your contact and tiptoe on the ice, you'll slip and slide all over and be miserable. When you step confidently, putting your weight squarely on it and believing you won't slip, you'll feel at home on the ice, and you'll look like you're at home. Make the suit your home."

He hiked up the belt and closed his eyes for a minute, trying to sink into the clothes. "I understand what you're saying. I'm just not used to working a look." He focused on relaxing for a few moments, then opened his eyes. "I was born to wear this suit," he said.

Blanchard clapped his hands. "That's it," he said. "Own it."

Lil Dove returned, carrying a toolbox of his own. "Can you take off the jacket and roll up your sleeve?" he asked, and Mason obeyed, draping the jacket carefully on the worktable so as not to reveal that his phone was inside. He unbuttoned his shirt cuff, and Lil Dove approached him with a handheld device that looked like the nozzle on Ned's garden hose. Before he could ask what was happening, Lil Dove tapped it on Mason's bare forearm.

"Ouch," he said, even though it had only stung a little. "What the hell was that?"

"Polio, smallpox, influenza H1N1, and a couple of other things."

"To prevent them, I hope, rather than induce them," he said, glaring at Lil Dove and rubbing the injection site.

Lil Dove laughed. "Trust me—you do not want to get polio."

"I might have been inoculated for it already," Mason said, annoyed that he hadn't even asked.

"You weren't. I checked."

"So, what, you phoned my doctor?"

"It would have shown up in your fluids," he said impatiently, putting the injector back in his toolbox.

Mason considered asking what the hell that meant, but he let it go. The technology here was advanced, he knew, but measuring him for a suit and checking his immunizations without him even noticing—its capabilities seemed limitless.

"Try the hat," Kitten said.

He picked it up and examined it to determine which end went at the front. He read the label sewn inside, and looked to Kitten for enlightenment: "'Mr. Pierre of Georgetown'?"

"The little bow goes at the back," she said.

"I know how hats work," he said, and set it on his head. Again, it fit really well. He pulled the jacket back on and stepped into the dressing room to look in the mirror. From a distance he wouldn't have even recognized himself.

"Money," Lil Dove said when he came back. He handed Mason a thick bundle of cash, folded in half. "That's eight hundred dollars."

Mason flipped through the stack, mostly fives and tens, in various states of wear. "Eight hundred?"

"Is it not enough? I could get more."

"I'm sure it's fine," he said. "It sounds like a lot of dough for then."

"Take off the trousers for a minute," Lil Dove said.

"More injections?" Mason asked, his eyes narrowing.

"No—I want to show you something."

It wasn't embarrassing at all to take them off, because the underpants were so baggy, thick, and high-waisted. He owned cargo shorts that were more revealing. He handed the pants to Lil Dove, who set them on the table.

"Feel the hem under the belt," he said, and Mason did. There were solid, thick disks sewn inside.

"Lead weights? In case I fall in a swimming pool?" he ventured.

"Even better," Lil Dove said, and with some difficulty worked a shiny gold coin out through an opening in the seam. "There are six of these."

Mason felt the pants again, sliding a pinky into an invisible pocket to feel one of the others. "Clever hiding place," he said, and took the coin from Lil Dove. It was inscribed CANADA, 24K, and TEN DOLLARS. On the back was the king's profile with GEORGIVS VI.

"The coins should be convertible anywhere, anytime," Lil Dove said. "They predate your travels, so they won't ever be an anachronism. Our thinking is that if your paper money gets stolen or mislaid, you'll likely still have your pants."

"It's a great idea," Mason said. "Is Qualtrough packing these too?"

"He didn't take any of the coins," Blanchard said. "Only cash."

"They're made of highly purified gold, so they're worth much more than ten Canadian dollars," Lil Dove said, meeting Mason's eye to make sure he understood.

"I actually know how that works too," he said, annoyed at the condescension.

"It's why Annette is letting him go," Blanchard said to Lil Dove. "He's practically from there. He doesn't need lessons."

Kitten took the coin and worked it back into the fabric of the trousers, and Mason pulled them back on.

When he'd finished tightening his belt, Lil Dove went back into his toolbox and handed Mason a little silver box.

"Flip it open with your thumb," he said.

Mason did, and a flame sprung up. "A lighter? Why would I need this?"

"Everyone had one," he said. "It's important in social interactions."

"I think you may have watched too many old movies," Mason said, but snapped it closed and slipped it into his pants pocket.

Next Lil Dove produced a black-and-white photo

141

of Qualtrough. It had a white border and a glossy finish, authentic to the era, and the image was closely cropped to obscure any clothing or background, save the top of his shirt collar. Mason looked at it for a moment, staring into his eyes, memorizing his features.

"You can show it to people when you're looking for him," Lil Dove explained.

"I wouldn't have thought of that," Mason said.

The sarcasm was lost on Lil Dove. "It's really the best way," he said earnestly. "It's easier than asking for him by name or trying to describe him."

"So much to remember," Mason muttered, and looked to Blanchard, who just grinned.

Lil Dove handed him a card of similar size that had a black-and-white photo of Mason affixed to it. It was a driver's license, dated 1952, issued by the District of Columbia. He ran his finger over the embossed seal.

"Where did you get my picture?" he asked.

"You're here, aren't you?" Lil Dove said.

Mason didn't reply but examined the license more closely. It was even timeworn around the edges, like the cash, as if it had been in his pocket for a while. He hated the way he looked in the photo, unsmiling and spaced-out. It was definitely him, although it had been taken before Kitten had oiled his hair. It might have been snapped in the bathroom mirror after a shower, but given his vapid blank stare, it could have been taken anywhere.

"Why did you use my real name?"

"Why not? It's easier to remember."

"Why D.C.?"

"Several reasons," Lil Dove said, leaning on the worktable. "California driving cards had no photo on them then, and having the photo gives it more gravity. It's also harder for the authorities to check on you, because that jurisdiction is across the country. Perhaps most important, it makes you an out-of-towner. It'll be easy for you to explain why you don't understand the local layout, in case you have to ask for a cobbler or a barbershop."

"I'm not going to be looking for those things," he said, and slipped the license and Qualtrough's photo into his jacket pocket next to his phone. "You've clearly put a lot of thought into this."

"We've spent years preparing for the exploration phase," Kitten said. "It'll be years before we get to implement it. You're seeing the fruit of a lot of time and effort."

"So who are you going to send through once you do it?"

"That hasn't been determined yet," she said. "It's a process."

"Has the plan always been to go to 1952?"

She hesitated, her eyes flicking to Blanchard. "That's classified."

"Fine," Mason said, frowning. "But I'm actually going, so maybe I should know some of this stuff."

"Two targets are being developed," Blanchard said, folding his arms. "Your time and the earlier time. For various technical reasons, both are stable points that we can connect to."

"How many people are you planning to send through?"

Blanchard raised his eyebrows. "I've said all I'm going to say."

"It seems odd that you people have so many secrets. You're working with ice cream money. I'll admit, it's really good ice cream. But I have to wonder, is this what the big boss wanted to do with all his money?"

"I can see why Annette thinks you'll do well there," Blanchard said. "You're ready and willing to break things."

"What are you talking about?"

"Your aggression. It sounds like you're threatening to contact Mr. Sarté because I won't tell you everything you want to know. That's an extreme overreaction."

"Is it?" Mason asked. He had to think about it. Maybe that was one of the cultural differences he felt with these people. They were so passive that they thought he was violent.

"Do you really need to know the full details of our program?" Blanchard asked, holding his gaze.

"No," Mason admitted.

"Then quit talking about it, and go find my boyfriend."

Lil Dove made a clicking sound with his tongue, and Kitten braced herself on the worktable. Both of them looked stunned.

"You're starting to sound just like him," Kitten said.

Blanchard grinned. "I like the way it feels. I guess

we're all just one atavism away from gang warfare."

Mason knew it was a reference to his world, their perception of his time as primitive and violent, but he didn't protest.

"Annette will be anxious to see us," Blanchard said. "If there's nothing else?"

Kitten shook her head, and Blanchard led them out into the corridor.

It felt strange to walk swathed in all the heavy fabric, but he leaned into it, like walking on ice, embracing it, and soon started to feel confident in his stride.

The machinery in the portal room was active, audibly at least, although there was no sign of the sphere, just the empty patch of floor at the front of the room. Blanchard joined Annette at the console, and Mason strolled around in front of it. He could feel his heart pounding. Maybe the low-frequency hum pervading the room was inducing unease, like Ned's vibrating-pipes theory.

"Are you feeling all right?" Annette asked.

He slid his hands into his pockets. "I think it's just being in this room. It makes it real."

"You look ready. It's startling how different you look from a few hours ago."

"That's all these two," Mason said, nodding to Kitten and Lil Dove.

"They do exacting work," Annette said, grinning at them.

"I truly appreciate the opportunity to be here to observe, Director," Kitten said quickly.

"Well, hopefully one day this will all be routine,"

Annette said. Turning to Blanchard, she asked, "How soon?"

"Minutes," he replied tersely, eyes glued to the controls on the console.

"I believe Blanchard explained that we're not certain what time of day it'll be when you arrive," Annette said.

"I know it's not perfect technology. I'll figure it out when I get there." Mason chuckled. "In my era people spend half their lives fighting with devices that barely work."

"Are you having second thoughts?" she asked. "That's your prerogative, of course."

Of course he was—what he was about to do was terrifying. But he took a deep breath and said, "Nope. I got through once—I'm not going to back out now. Let's light it up."

"Full conformity," Blanchard said, still fixated on the console. "Ready when you are."

"Right," Annette said, taking a firm tone. "Step through the portal quickly, and try to avoid the edges of the opening."

"I've done this before, remember?"

"Stand inside the green lines, with your back to us," Blanchard said.

Mason looked to the stretch of floor where he'd tumbled out of the sphere, and sure enough a green box, just big enough to fit the soles of his shoes, had lit up in the floor. He stepped over and took his place inside it, facing the racks of machinery, then twisted to look over his shoulder.

"Ready," he called to them.

The familiar high-pitched whine filled the room, almost deafening for a few seconds and then quieter. The sphere blew up out of nothing right in front of him. He fought the instinct to step back. Inside it he could see into a dark room, illuminated only by the white light from the room he was standing in. He could see plain walls, and the end of an old-fashioned single bed.

He turned back one last time, forced a nonchalant smile, and called to them, "I'll be right back."

His heart pounding, he took a deep breath and stepped out of the green box, into the portal, ducking his head and carefully lifting his feet over the strobing edge.

EIGHT

The floor must have been at a slightly different angle, because he stumbled and fell onto one knee. The sphere shrank to nothing with a shriek, and he stood up, rubbing his leg, the sudden silence striking.

He was standing in a dark and dingy room, with a single bed in an iron frame, a lone hardback chair, and a dresser. The wooden floors were either unfinished or had lost their varnish long ago. There was a lot of open floor space, he realized, like Yoshida's room 203. It made sense that Annette would have found a place with enough room to open the sphere.

Daylight streamed through thin curtains, but when he pulled them aside the window only provided a close-up view of the clapboard wall of the building next door. At least he could see it was daytime. He glanced in the closet, but there wasn't any evidence of Qualtrough or anyone else, just a couple of empty wire hangers. The bed was made up, but when he slid open the dresser drawers, there was nothing in them.

He looked around, taking it in. He knew he had to leave this room. It was intimidating, and he hadn't thought much about what it would actually feel like to be here, but it was exciting too, like he was about to visit a really good museum. With a few deep breaths, he spent a minute psyching himself into the right frame of mind. He couldn't gawk like a tourist out there—he had to lean into it, like walking on a skating rink. You're here, he told himself. Be here.

He unlocked the deadbolt and pulled open the door. The room was at the end of a long hall, with daylight visible through the glass of the front door at the other end. Several other doors lined the hall. Maybe it was a hotel or a rooming house. He noticed one of them, near the front, was ajar. Be confident, he reminded himself, and set off, walking like he knew where he was.

In the open doorway stood a bone-thin woman, gray hair pulled back into a bun, an apron over her print dress. She looked worried.

Mason paused and greeted her warmly. "How are you?"

"I thought I heard something going on back there. How do you fellas get in that room?" she demanded. "I didn't hear you come in."

"Are you the manager?"

"Don't act so surprised," she snapped. "Lots of ladies have jobs like this."

"I'm not surprised," he said, flustered by her reaction. He pulled nervously at his open jacket.

"Did my son give you the key?"

"My friend did," Mason said, thinking quickly.

"He didn't tell me he'd be having so many guests."

"Who's been here?"

She frowned. "You're awfully nosy."

"I don't mean to be rude," he said gently. "I'm actually looking for my friend." He pulled the photo of Qualtrough out of his inner pocket and handed it to her.

She hesitated, looking at the photo but not reaching for it, leaning away. But curiosity overcame her reticence. She took the photo and peered at it, then frowned as she handed it back.

"I thought you said he gave you the key."

"When did you last see him?"

She didn't answer, glancing down at his shoes to assess him before meeting his gaze, suspicion in her eyes.

The film noir detective would have pressured her to get answers, Mason thought. He tried a line that Buster had used, mimicking his hard intonation. "Sing, sister," he said, glaring at her. "I ain't got all day."

She looked alarmed, but it worked.

"He's the one who took the room," she said quickly. "He paid for the whole month, but I haven't seen him for a few days."

"Now, wasn't that easy?" He grinned. "Do you

151

have any idea where he might have gone?"

"None. I saw him with a blond-haired gentleman on Thursday."

"So that's ... four days ago?" he ventured.

"Thursday," she repeated, perplexed. "Two days ago."

"Right," Mason said. "What did the blond look like?"

"Not nearly as tall as you. Slightly built, good-looking. Impeccable manners. A real Southern gentleman."

He nodded. "I appreciate your candor. Do you know what time it is now?"

"Five-thirty. Time for my supper."

"I'll leave you to it, then," he said, and walked toward the front door. Her supper couldn't have been that urgent, as he felt her watching him walk away.

"Did you come here just to toss his room?" she called after him, more strident now that he was far enough away for her to slam her door on him if necessary.

"I didn't toss anything," he called to her, not bothering to turn around. "I'll be back—I'm staying until I find him."

"That's a single room," she said.

He looked back as he opened the front door. "And I'm the single occupant until he shows up."

She frowned, unsure whether that sounded right or not.

"Cool it, toots," he said, channeling Buster again. "It's all gonna be fine."

Her eyebrows shot up, and he left without waiting for a response. It seemed reasonable to plan to sleep here, given that she'd already seen his face. It gave him access to the room, and besides, Qualtrough had already paid her for it.

Stepping outside and descending the building's front steps, he strolled along the sidewalk, trying not to rubberneck but startled by the environment. Ancient hulking cars lined the street, and they came in a riot of colors. He hadn't expected that. In old black-and-white photos they were always shades of gray. There were a lot of people around, the men dressed like he was, every one of them wearing a hat, and the women dressed like the rooming house manager, modest dresses and skirts, clunky shoes.

The houses lining the narrow street were Victorians, and at the corner the cross-street dropped sharply away, down a steep grade. He couldn't think of any neighborhood in LA that looked like this, and for a minute he wondered if they had deposited him in San Francisco instead. Annette and her team had blown it with Yoshida's building, thinking it was abandoned, and the building he'd just stepped into wasn't empty either, so it wasn't a stretch to think they'd pointed the sphere at the wrong city.

But based on the suits and the cars, they had gotten the timing right, so maybe it didn't matter exactly where he was. Most important, Qualtrough was here—the manager had recognized him.

Walking up the block, the street sign at the next corner looked familiar. In the same style the city still used in his era, it read 2ND ST, and then it struck him: this was Bunker Hill, right downtown, before it had been razed and flattened and stacked with sterile glass office towers. He grinned and looked down the slope, the street much steeper here than in his version, and absent of anything tall or shiny. He recognized a couple of the buildings off in the original financial district. They were high-end condo conversions in his era, and presumably still office buildings here, but they were the same—this was definitely Los Angeles.

Turning right at the corner, he walked the length of the block, then the next one, taking in the people, the cars, the atmosphere. It was familiar and startlingly alien by turns—many women wore their hair gray, so they looked older than they really were, and every single man was wearing a hat, even the guy cutting a lawn with a mechanical push mower, wearing grubby work clothes with a matching cap. Strolling the streets of the neighborhood, he had to smile—he'd made it; he was here.

Eventually he decided he'd done enough sightseeing—he needed a plan. Retracing his steps, he thought about his quarry. If Qualtrough had paid for that room, he was planning to come back to it. He found the house again, following a husky guy in a brown suit up the front steps. A sign mounted beside the front door read NO ROOMS. That and the lack of any signage implied it was a rooming house rather than a hotel.

The lodger took out a key and opened one of the other doors in the hallway. Mason said "Hello" as he walked past, and the guy responded with a grunt and a suspicious look before quickly closing his door. Qualtrough's room was unlocked and empty, just as he'd left it.

He snapped the ceiling light on, took off his hat, and looked around. The space was depressing. He hung his jacket and his hat on the hooks on the back of the door and stretched out on the bed, not bothering to take off his shoes. The whole thing, the search, seemed overwhelming, and he didn't even know where to start.

The glare of the bare bulb was annoying, and he was staring right at it. Maybe waiting here wasn't such a good idea. It felt oppressive, and there was a persistent smell, something like machine oil or furniture polish. He realized he wasn't going to be able to stay here for long, not if he wanted to stay sane.

He had other tools—tuning in with his psychic power might give him a lead. He closed his eyes and was starting the process of clearing his head when the dresser flashed into his mind. The drawers had been empty when he'd done a cursory search. Or had they?

He got up and opened the top drawer, then the second, and found it—a plain little notepad, small enough to fit in a shirt pocket. It hadn't really registered before. Maybe he'd been checking for clothes, or still regaining his balance after stepping out of the institute. But he was holding it in his hands now, and someone had written on the top sheet.

The printing was blocky and childish, done in hard pencil: a list of three names and street addresses.

He knew all three were downtown, and if his memory of the numbering was right, all were within a block or two of Pershing Square. They sounded like restaurants: Chez Henri, The Anvil, Blue Moon Lounge. He sat on the bed and studied the faint list. Not restaurants, he decided—bars.

Had Qualtrough written this? He was the current tenant of this sad dump, but the handwriting didn't look like that of a futuristic scientist. In each listing the word *Street* was abbreviated "Str.," which felt like something a nonnative speaker would do. Seventh Street was written with a slash in it, "7/th," which seemed downright bizarre.

He closed his eyes for a second and imagined Qualtrough writing on the pad. These had to be places he went, or wanted to go. It wouldn't take long to scope out all three—they were right down the hill. It was certainly a more appealing prospect than sitting here.

He tore off the sheet and threw the pad back in the dresser drawer. When he stuffed the list in his pants pocket, he felt the bulge of the lighter and the wad of money Lil Dove had given him. He pulled it out, split the stack in two, and put half back in his pants. For the rest, there had to be a good hiding place in the room. He looked under the bed, but the steel frame was completely exposed, with nothing between it and the mattress. He pulled one of the dresser drawers all the way out, but there was no frame behind it; if he put the bills back there, they would just fall to the floor. The closet was tiny and unlit, but when he reached up toward the ceiling inside above the doorway, he could feel the unfinished wooden slats of the wall, held together with rough plaster. He pried one of the slats away from the plaster, as high up as he could reach, and pinned the wad of bills behind it. No one else would find it without a flashlight and a chair to stand on. He reached behind his back and felt the gold coins under his belt. They were already well hidden, and he decided to leave them be. If he got robbed, he had a stash of cash back here, and as Lil Dove had said, it was unlikely anyone would take his pants.

He'd let the manager assume he had a key to the room, but now he wished he really did. Hopefully no casual interloper would be able to find his stash. Putting on his jacket and hat, he quietly closed the door behind him.

It was hard to tell what time of year it was, based on the weather, but he guessed it was April. The sun was already setting as he strolled back toward Second Street, so it wasn't midsummer, and the air had that mild spring vibe, after the winter rains but before the gloomy overcast days of May and June.

Trotting down the staircase that led down the hill, he soaked in the city's atmosphere. Bunker Hill was new to him in its current state, but down here, it felt odd to walk on streets that were familiar in places and then completely foreign. He marveled at the crowds of people, so uniform in their dress, the cramped little shops, the smell of diesel soot in the air, the noisy vehicles lumbering past. Any romantic notion he'd had of a glamorous stroll through this era was dissipating in the face of the gritty reality.

Pershing Square was where it should have been, but it looked completely different, with shade trees and pleasant walkways, and it was easy to get into, no parking-lot ramps dividing it from the rest of the city. He cut through the middle of the greenery, observing the couples crowded on the benches, chatting and people-watching. His grandparents could be among them, he thought with a shudder, young and randy and enjoying the evening air. Occasionally someone would catch his eye, but no one looked at him like he didn't belong. Kitten had done an excellent job.

His first stop was The Anvil. The address led him into a dead-end alley off Seventh Street, and he found a door emblazoned with the right number, but it wasn't marked with a sign. It looked more like a fire exit than a place of business. He tried the door handle, but it was locked. If Qualtrough had been looking for where the guys were, as Louie had implied, this was the right kind of place—below the radar, out of sight to anyone but those in the know. He pounded on the door, but it was heavy, and unlikely that anyone inside would even hear him. It was still early evening. Maybe he'd try later.

The next closest place was the Blue Moon Lounge, not far away. The address written on the pad was 482½, and he found a hat shop at 482, right beside 484, with nothing between them but a thick wall. He stood near the curb for a minute, next to a parking meter, looking up and down the block, trying to assess whether Qualtrough had written it down wrong or if another nearby doorway might be the right one.

Grinning broadly, a guy stopped and asked him, "Are you looking for the burley-cue?"

"What's a burley-cue?" Mason asked.

"You know—dancing girls," he said, and winked. He rarely saw anyone do that, and from this guy it felt especially louche. No wonder it had gone out of style.

"I'm actually looking for a place called the Blue Moon Lounge," Mason said.

The guy's face clouded. "I don't know anything about that," he said.

"Are you sure?" Mason asked. It must be close, if the guy recognized the name—and he obviously did, despite his denial.

"Spread out," he said, his voice low, almost threatening, and quickly continued on his way.

Mason watched him walk away. Spreading out would be difficult, considering he was alone, but maybe it had another meaning. And what was a burley-queue? He thought about the word, wondered how it was spelled. It took him a minute, but he figured it out: it was a mangled pronunciation of *burlesque*. The fact that winking man was repulsed by mention of the Blue Moon Lounge suddenly felt like a good sign—if it was even less reputable than a strip

159

joint, maybe it was indeed a gay bar.

He walked around the corner, but the numbers here were completely different, aligned with the cross street. There was an alley a few yards down, though, and he walked into it, up to the point where he estimated he was at the back of the millinery. There were a couple of nondescript fire doors in the brick wall, spaced a few yards apart and surrounded by old-fashioned trash cans, but none of them were marked. He stood for a minute, inspecting them, and saw that the fraction ½ appeared in faded black paint above one of the doors. His pulse quickened. This might be it.

He tried the door handle—it was unlocked. A cloud of tobacco smoke billowed into his face when he pulled it open. There was a small landing and a flight of stairs leading down, with another landing near the bottom. He couldn't see inside from the doorway, but he could hear voices below. He pulled the door closed behind him and started down the steps.

It was definitely a drinking establishment, with a long old-school bar running the length of the room. There were a few guys sitting at the bar, and eight or ten people at tables. Every eyeball in the place was locked on him the moment he stepped in. It was disconcerting, but he feigned calm composure, grinning and stepping up to the bar. The lighting was low, but looking around, it struck him that everyone in the place was white and Anglo. At a cursory glance, he couldn't tell if the few women he saw had been born that way or not.

This was definitely where the guys were—and that meant the list had to be Qualtrough's. The room had fallen silent, and Mason felt his cheeks burning, knowing that his presence was the cause. Most of the patrons were watching him with unmasked suspicion. Where was the damn bartender? Mason sat on a barstool and swiveled away from the room, peering through the arched doorway into the back, willing someone to appear.

Someone soon did, stepping through the archway—an older guy, completely bald, wearing the traditional white shirt and dark vest of his profession. He was solidly built, arm muscles rippling in his shirtsleeves. He probably handled the bouncing on his own.

"This is a members-only club," he said, frowning at Mason.

"All right—how much will a membership cost me?" Mason asked.

The guy folded his arms. "Ten dollars."

"I'd be happy to buy in. I'm meeting a friend here later." He dug in his pocket and pulled out a few bills, folding a ten lengthwise and setting it on the bar. "There's my fee, and here's five to get my tab started," he said, putting it beside the ten.

The barman picked up the ten, leaving the five, but he looked wary. "Is your friend a club member?"

"I think so."

"What's his name?"

"Dorothy," he said clearly, so that he could easily

be overheard. "I'm a friend of Dorothy."

The barman raised his eyebrows, but he didn't look convinced. "What are you drinking?"

"What kind of beer are you trying to get rid of?"

"The Kronenbourg."

"I'll take a bottle of that."

The bartender stepped into the back, and Mason surreptitiously looked around the room. The tension had subsided, the guys going back to their conversations, only a few beady eyes on him now. The handful of women in the joint hadn't always been women, he saw now, and were definitely working drag. It was subtle, though, not like the exaggerated and glammy drag Mason knew. From a distance or in low light they could easily pass. One of the patrons, alone at the other end of the bar, caught his eye, and Mason grinned and winked at her, channeling the sleazeball he'd met on the street.

The bartender returned and put a little card and a pen in front of Mason, then set down a bottle of Kronenbourg and a glass. He picked up the five and said, "May I take your hat?"

He'd forgotten he was wearing it. He pulled it off and handed it across the bar. The bartender took it, then set it down at Mason's elbow with a pointed look. Leaving it on was probably a faux pas, he realized, as nobody else had one on. He spotted the other men's hats hung on a rack near the stairs.

Ignoring the glass and drinking a slug of beer from the bottle, he picked up the little card. It was emblazoned across the top with BLUE MOON LOUNGE and a big blue dot, presumably representing the full moon. Below that it read,

> This is to certify that ____ is a member in good standing for the year ending ____ .

There was a place for his signature and that of the "Secretary." He filled in the space with his name and scrawled his signature below, leaving the year for the barman to write in, as he wasn't sure what year it actually was. He slid the card and the pen back across the bar.

A lot of the patrons were smoking, and it was starting to irritate his eyes. A matchbook sat in the ashtray in front of him on the bar. He picked it up to find it had the same blue dot logo, without the name, just the word "TRinity" followed by five numbers. It took him a moment to parse it: it was an old-timey phone number. He lifted the cover and examined the neat little row of paper matches. He'd seen these before, but only as a curious artifact in the antiques section at the flea market. He folded it closed again and tucked it into his pocket, thinking the phone number might come in useful at some point.

The bartender came back and set his change on the bar, four singles and some coins, then picked up the membership card and examined it. "Mr. Braith-waite," he said, glancing up at Mason. "That doesn't sound made up."

"It's not. Do you want to see my ID?"

He chuckled. "No. It's just that we get a lot of Smiths and Joneses in here. I'll get this back to you in a minute." He slipped the card into his breast pocket.

The drag queen he'd winked at got off her stool, casually smoothing the front of her pink skirt, and made her way over to Mason. Her confident gait in spike heels made it look like she'd been born in them. She stood beside his stool at the bar, almost too close. Maybe that wink had been unwise. At such close range he saw that her wig was good—he couldn't tell where the faux brunette curls met the real thing. Her flowery perfume overpowered even the tobacco smoke.

"Buy a girl a drink?" she asked.

"What are you drinking?" he asked, and turned toward her on his stool, his knee brushing her skirt. It was a perfect way to make connections in this place, being invited into a conversation—even better than buying a membership.

"Gin and tonic."

It was easy to catch the bartender's eye—the place wasn't that busy, and he seemed to be keeping an eye on Mason.

"A G and T for the lady," Mason said, then realized the guy might not recognize the abbreviation.

But the barman just nodded and stepped away.

She was grinning at him, and looking him over, which was completely unnerving. He tried to look suave but he knew he was blushing. At least it wouldn't be too obvious in the dim light of the barroom.

"What's your name?" he asked her.

"Mamie."

"That's a pretty name," he said. "Pleased to meet you, ma'am. I'm Mason."

"Miss," she said reproachfully, and gently slapped his forearm.

"Excuse me?"

"Not ma'am. That sounds like my grandmother. Miss."

"Forgive me, miss," he said.

The barman set down a highball glass and deftly took a bill from the pile of change.

Mamie tilted the glass briefly toward Mason and then delicately sipped from the straw, watching him while she playfully rolled one shoulder, then the other. Mason smiled and took a pull of his beer.

"So what are you doing here?" she asked finally. "You don't look like any friend of Dorothy's that I ever saw."

"What do Dorothy's friends usually look like?"

"Scared, when they first show up here. You don't look scared."

"I guess it's because you put me at ease, Mamie."

She snorted and set down her glass. "I'm sure there's more to it."

Mason considered pulling out Qualtrough's photo, but decided to let the conversation progress first. Despite playing the coquette, Mamie was suspicious of him.

Instead he said, "I'm looking for a guy."

"Maybe I'm that guy," she said, and held his gaze with a come-hither look. She leaned closer, pressing against his inner thigh, her blood-red lips slightly parted.

"I don't usually kiss girls," Mason said gently. He

leaned back a little, but didn't move his leg, letting her put her weight on it.

"I'm not really a girl," she said. "I'm a boy in a dress."

"Whatever you say."

She leaned in, kissing him on the mouth.

Mason tensed up for a second but then went with it, relaxed into it, got lost in it. It had been so long since he'd kissed anyone but Ned. He felt a fleeting flash of guilt—how was he going to explain this to Ned? Right now, though, it was kind of great. He put a hand on her shoulder, felt the thin silky fabric of her sleeve, the unfeminine musculature beneath.

After what seemed like forever, she pulled away, and perched on the next barstool.

"You're a pretty good kisser," she said matter-of-factly.

Mason felt dazed, but Mamie seemed even more focused than before.

"Do you kiss all the new members like that?" he asked.

"Only the shady ones."

The bartender stepped over, a broad smile on his face, and handed him a tissue.

Mason took it, asking, "What's this for?"

"You disturbed the lady's makeup." He discreetly tapped his own lips. "The name is Gus, by the way," he said, before moving down the bar.

Mason wiped his mouth with the tissue. A startling amount of red came off. "What is this stuff?" he asked.

Mamie chuckled. "Crimson Carnage." She'd pulled a lipstick tube out of her handbag and was carefully doing a touch-up, looking at herself in a little compact mirror.

Mason surreptitiously watched her work, fascinated and a little turned on.

The room grew louder as a couple of new faces descended the stairs, boisterously greeted by their friends. The bartender served them farther down the bar, and Mason watched the interaction.

"Is Gus a friend of yours? He's certainly changed his tune with me."

Mamie shrugged. "Now he knows you're not a cop." She snapped her compact shut and dropped it into her handbag.

Mason considered that. Everyone in the bar had been suspicious of him, worried that he might be a threat. Now they were happily ignoring him. A cop probably would have called in his colleagues with billy clubs, or started arresting the boys in dresses.

"Mamie, you are so fierce," Mason said.

She tilted her head. "What do you mean?"

"You kissed me, even though you thought I might be a cop. The way the world is today, a cop would have split your head open if you tried that. You're very brave."

"Thank you, Red," she said, smiling at the compliment. "But it was just a kiss. It didn't mean anything."

He sighed. Maybe not to her, he thought, but it meant he had some explaining to do when he got home.

"Can I show you a photo?" he asked, pulling it out of his pocket.

Mamie took it and examined it, holding it up to get better light.

"He's quite a looker."

"Have you seen him?"

"Is he a friend of yours?" she asked, eyeing him and handing the photo back.

"I'm working for his boyfriend. He took off a while ago, and we're trying to track him down."

"What will you do if you find him?"

"Encourage him to come home with me."

She nodded. "Where's home?"

"Back east. Vermont."

She sipped her drink and watched him for a minute before she spoke. "And you're not looking to rough him up or shake him down."

He smiled. "I'm not. I'm telling the truth."

"I think I might actually believe you." She pulled a cigarette out of her bag and delicately held it aloft, looking at him expectantly.

It took him a second to realize she wanted him to light it. He dug into his pants pocket and found the lighter, flipping it open and holding it up as she sucked on the end to get it burning. Lil Dove had been right about that, he thought, snapping it shut. It served as a social lubricant.

"I'm smart, you know," she said, turning her head to blow the smoke away from him. "I might not look it, but I am."

"That doesn't surprise me at all."

"I've got people smarts, and I'm a pretty good judge of character. You seem like a decent guy, Red, so I'll put it to you straight." She took another drag on her cigarette, watching him. "He's been in here, but he's mixed up with a lowlife. When did he go missing?"

Mason thought for a minute. "Earlier this week. Maybe Tuesday."

She sipped her drink and nodded. "I saw him in here Wednesday night. Same jazz as you—dropped a sawbuck like it was chump change. And no fear, either. Vermont must be an enlightened place."

"What did you mean by a lowlife? Who was he with?"

"A guy named Leslie. I saw the whole thing, from the first pass to the pickup. It was like watching a rube getting fleeced in a clip joint. Your friend was a real pushover. I wondered if he wasn't maybe a bit simple."

"Not simple," Mason said. "Just innocent." He drank a mouthful of his beer. "Is Leslie blond? Slender?"

"That's him. He slinks around like a peroxide weasel. He's got a Southern accent too, but I think it might be fake."

"Have you seen him since Wednesday?"

"Leslie, sure—he's here every night. But not your friend. He was only in here the one time. What's his name?"

"Qualtrough," Mason said grimly. "Has Leslie been in tonight?"

"He comes around late, but he always comes around."

"Maybe he'll be at The Anvil."

She shook her head. "Leslie doesn't go there. You shouldn't bother—they're a bunch of sissies."

Mason glanced down at her skirt, raising his eyebrows.

"You know what I mean—it's the rowdy crowd. Tequila shots and bathtub gin. People here know how to behave, but at The Anvil they're swinging from the chandeliers. I used to go, but after the third or fourth time waking up with no memory of the previous evening, I moved over here."

That actually sounded like it might be fun—the rowdiness, not getting blackout drunk—but fun wasn't why Mason was here. "Why do you say Leslie is a con man?"

"He runs scams," she said simply.

"Like what?"

"I've heard he's blackmailed married men, and people in government jobs. Guys who have a lot to lose and are willing to pay to protect it. I avoid him, but there are always new faces, new marks." She stubbed out her cigarette in the ashtray. "Like your friend Qualtrough."

Mason had a sinking feeling in the pit of his stomach.

The bartender came by and handed him the membership card. "Thank you for your patronage, Mr. Braithwaite."

"Thanks, Gus. Call me Mason." He examined

the card. There was a scribbled signature now on the line for "Secretary," and according to Gus, it was definitely 1952.

"So what time is late?" Mason asked Mamie, draining his beer.

"You mean when Leslie shows up? After eleven."

"I'll be back then. Maybe I'll see you."

"Unless I meet Prince Charming first," she said, flipping her hair and flashing him a vampish smile.

He picked up his change, leaving Gus a dollar bill. It didn't seem like a lot, but it was a fat tip considering what Mason had spent on booze—he had more than three bucks in change from the five. He chuckled and slipped it into his pocket, then stood up and headed toward the stairs.

"Do you want your hat?" Gus called after him.

He turned back. "I forgot."

It was still sitting on the bar, and Gus picked it up and handed it to him, a bemused look on his face.

It was dark when Mason stepped out into the alley, but there were plenty of people around when he reached the street. He needed to eat, but he hadn't thought about how to make that happen in a time before vegan was a thing. The central market would be closed by now. Among the handful of places he knew that dated back to this era, the best option was Clifton's, a cafeteria where he could see what he was getting up front.

It was just a few blocks away. Navigating the crowds of people, he felt more at home now, caught up in the energy of the city, no longer gawking like he was at a costume party. He thought about the Blue Moon and everything Mamie had told him. She knew a lot, he realized in retrospect, and it was excellent luck that he'd found Qualtrough's notes—it had saved him a lot of research time. Qualtrough hadn't been to the Blue Moon since Wednesday, and the rooming house manager hadn't seen him since Thursday. More than two days. Anything could have happened to him. He needed to find Leslie.

Broadway glittered with neon, and the sidewalks here were even more crowded. Bright department store windows lined the street, and people were shopping—there was nothing of the grungy and down-market Broadway he knew. Streetcars ran in both directions, vehicles dodging them, pedestrians hustling to get off the tracks. He stopped on the sidewalk for a minute to watch, hands in his pockets. People boarded and disembarked the lumbering beast, then its doors closed and it rolled away. It was such a good idea, so smooth and roomy compared to buses. Getting rid of them hadn't been an improvement.

Clifton's looked much the same, an island of stability in the roiling sea of change, just as dusty and timeworn as his version. It was popular—he had to wait in line with a horde of enthusiastic diners, sliding their trays along and craning to view the dubious comestibles on the steam tables. He asked for a double order of the carrot side dish—carrots cut into little cubes and mixed with peas—and he took two apples. Everything else was swimming in butter or flecked with ham. He grabbed a coffee too and found a little table on one of the elevated paths in the dining room, a few steps above the main floor, replete with its taxidermy fauna, faux trees, and animatronic forest creatures.

He remembered to take his hat off as he sat down, and ate his overcooked veggies while watching the other diners, enthralled with their idiosyncrasies. They looked so different on the surface, but the suits and dresses were just as much drag as the look Mamie was working. Underneath they were still people, chatting and laughing and flirting over their high-cholesterol meals.

He finished the apples and sipped his coffee, closing his eyes to listen to the din of the room. He could feel the entire frenetic city rotating around him, loud and grimy and rough. He was tired, he realized, and overstimulated. He put on his hat and went back out to the street, walking up Broadway, then on the side streets, admiring the familiar architecture and appreciating the quieter space in front of shuttered banks and office buildings. He walked through Pershing Square again, its benches under the palm trees still crowded in the nighttime, which made it feel safer, and eventually made his way back to the Blue Moon.

NINE

us caught his eye and greeted him warmly as he descended the stairs. The place was a lot more crowded now, and louder. A young man was behind the bar helping Gus, pulling beer from the tap. Mason hung his hat with the others and scanned the faces, looking for a skinny blond, barely able to see through the tobacco smoke.

Mamie waved to him from a table, where she sat with some friends, two of them dressed like boys and two like girls. She gestured toward the end of the bar, where she'd been sitting earlier, and he met her there, climbing onto a stool beside her. She leaned in close and spoke in hushed tones, like an old confidant.

"Leslie's been in," she said.

"Damn it. I missed him."

"Oh, he'll be back. It was just an early recon mission."

Gus stopped in front of them and asked, "Kronenbourg?"

"Sounds great," Mason said, and to Mamie, "For the lady?"

"No, thanks," she said, gesturing vaguely to the table where she'd been sitting. "I'm already working on one."

When Gus had gone, Mason asked her, "Was he with anyone?"

"He was alone—no sign of your handsome friend."

"Thanks for keeping your eyes peeled," he said. "I guess I'll wait for Leslie. If you see him, will you point him out to me?"

"I don't think you'll miss him. But I'll keep you company until he shows up. Once I spot him, I'll scram. You won't have to do anything—he'll be all over you."

Gus set his beer on the bar, and Mason scrabbled in his pants for a dollar, handing it across to him.

"I don't want to keep you from your friends," Mason told Mamie.

She snorted. "They're always here. It's much more fun to be tangled up in detective intrigue. You are a detective, aren't you?"

"I don't have a license or anything, but I guess I kind of am."

"Honey, you need to sell it," she said. "Repeat after me: I'm a detective."

176

"I'm a detective," Mason said.

"Good, but butch it up a bit." Her voice dropped two octaves: "I'm a detective."

He thought about Buster, and said it the way he would: gruffly, narrowing his eyes, looking sidelong at Mamie. "I'm a detective."

"Yes," she said, laughing and gently touching his forearm. "I'm quaking in my pumps."

"Sell it. That's good advice," he said, and tipped his bottle to her before taking a drink.

"I didn't spill the beans about that, by the way," she said.

"You mean what I'm really doing here?"

"That you're looking to talk to Leslie. I didn't want to tip him off."

"Thanks," Mason said, surprised. He hadn't even considered the possibility.

"Some of these hens were gossiping about the fresh meat, but I didn't say anything. So Leslie knows about you, but not that you know about him."

"You really are on the ball, Mamie."

"I know how to keep things quiet. I was in military intelligence."

"During the war?"

"Ah-yup. That's where I learned to wear a dress. Were you in the service?"

"No," Mason said, but looked up when Mamie grabbed his forearm, her fingers grasping tightly.

She didn't say anything, because she didn't have to—Leslie had just come down the stairs. She got up, wordlessly, and recovered her drink from the table

177

where her friends were, then daintily took a solitary stool halfway down the bar, her back to the room.

Leslie hung his flashy camel-hair overcoat and hat near the stairs, and within moments had spotted Mason, a glint in his eye. Mason returned his gaze, but Leslie quickly looked away, nonchalantly making his way to the other end of the bar. The game was on.

Mason knew the type: so good-looking they get spoiled by the attention. The downside was the gradual decline—as they got older and their looks started to fade, they slowly went mad as the ardor of others waned but their own expectations didn't. Leslie looked to be a few years down that path, still playing the part of the hottest guy in the bar, but with the inevitable controlled desperation setting in.

Leslie paid Gus for a tumbler of something and stood alone, casually surveying the room. Mason knew he was the fresh meat, and as Mamie had said, all he had to do was wait. Leslie took the stool beside Mamie, where he could talk to her but subtly appraise Mason, maybe even flirt with him. He reclined against the bar, facing the room, and glanced Mason's way as he spoke to Mamie. Mason didn't hear what he said to her, but her response was loud.

"Beat it, chump. You're a wrong guy."

Leslie stood up again, thoroughly offended, and surveyed the bar, considering his options. He looked toward Mason, calculating whether or not he should approach or defer. Mason nodded in greeting, and Leslie made his decision—he came over.

Mamie caught Mason's eye and winked, then

took her drink and went back to her friends. If she'd planned that, it was incredibly strategic—she'd quickly delivered Leslie into his lap, and even rattled him a little so that Mason could see through his cunning.

Leslie sat on the stool beside Mason and set his tumbler on the bar. Up close, he looked even older than he had from across the room, but he was still devilishly handsome. He spoke to Mason like they were old friends.

"Watch out for that sissy," he said. "He's an ornery one." His Southern dialect was pronounced—the word sounded like "*awn*-reh."

Mason chuckled. "She dresses girly, but she could probably kick my ass. She was in the military." He made a point of looking Leslie over. "She could definitely kick your ass."

Leslie scoffed. "He wouldn't know where to start with me. He's as common as mud."

"We're all common," Mason said. "This country doesn't have any nobility, last time I checked."

"Not that kind of common," Leslie said, frowning. "I mean that he dresses like a girl. I'm quite properly a gentleman, and I act like one."

"What's wrong with dressing like a girl? Mamie's really good at it. She's more stable in those heels than I am in bare feet."

"I heard that he kissed you," Leslie said, insistent. "All I'm saying is, don't mix with him, or people will think y'all are one of them."

"I have a lot more in common with her than with

you," Mason said, and drank from his beer bottle.

Leslie sighed and ran a hand through his slick hair. Mamie was wrong about the blond coming out of a bottle, Mason thought—he was blond to the roots.

"I've forgotten my manners," Leslie said, the edge gone from his voice, his drawl again more pronounced. "That sissy threw me off. Leslie," he said, extending his hand.

He shook it briefly and said, "Mason."

"So, Mr. Mason, I heard that y'all have money," Leslie said. "I'm sick of the regular slobs around here. I'm a simple Southern gentleman, with simple desires, and I'd like to spend some time with a quality specimen like you."

He was surprised at the frank approach. "I don't really have money."

He arched his back and smiled. "Y'all aren't from around here, are you, Stretch?" he said, taking a sip from his glass, the ice rattling.

Mason watched him for a moment. That smile, and the light in his eyes—Mason could see how easy seduction was for him. He knew it was part of a con, but the logical thing to do was to let it play out.

"Yes and no," he said. "Where are you from?"

"As I said, I trace my roots to the South."

"Bakersfield South, or Dixie South?" Mason asked.

"Bakersfield?"

"Lots of people around B-field sound like you. They moved there during the Depression."

"I'm not from Bakersfield," he said. "I was born in the heart of Dixie."

"And now?"

"I live in Toluca Lake."

"I know where that is," Mason said. He was enjoying this, knowing what Leslie wanted without him knowing that he knew. It felt good to needle him a little. "Isn't it kind of far?"

"Well, this is where the gentlemen are," he said, gesturing to the barroom. "You can get there by streetcar, but I drive. Once they finish building out the freeway system, it'll be minutes from here, day or night."

"I wouldn't hold my breath on that one."

Leslie pulled a little gold case out of his inside jacket pocket and popped it open, revealing a row of trim white cigarettes.

"No, thanks," Mason said when Leslie offered him one. This time he was ready, and had the lighter out by the time Leslie had tucked away his case, a cigarette dangling from his lips.

After he'd got the thing burning and Mason had pocketed his lighter, Leslie notched the cigarette between his fingers, one elbow on the bar, and turned toward him. His chin down, he looked up at Mason, his eyes soft, intent. Here was the come-on.

"I like you, Stretch. I really do."

Mason held his gaze. "I'm glad. Where's Qualtrough?"

Leslie reacted like an electric shock had run through him. Fear flashed in his eyes, but he quickly regained his composure.

"I don't know who you're talking about," he said, his accent slipping, and stubbed out his barely burned cigarette in an ashtray. He picked up his tumbler, preparing to stand.

"Don't you fucking move," Mason growled.

Leslie froze.

"Look at me," Mason demanded, keeping his voice low.

Leslie obeyed, naked fear in his eyes now.

"I know you were with him, here and at the place on Clay Street. So sing."

"I do remember that name," he said quickly, "now that I think on it. We must have met here. But I certainly don't know where he is."

"Leslie," Mason said intently, "you're right about me. I'm not a regular slob. I'm your worst fucking nightmare, and I'm not going to take your bullshit."

Leslie looked shocked. "I don't want trouble."

"Then tell me what happened to Qualtrough."

"I heard he got pinched a couple of days ago. In Pershing Square."

"When?"

"Thursday. That's all I know."

"You were there?"

He hesitated, his eyes flicking around the bar. "I was."

"What did he get pinched for?"

"I assume the charge is lewd conduct."

"How did you avoid getting caught?"

"I knew enough to run." He swirled his drink

and then slammed it, setting the tumbler down with a clatter. "Listen," he whined. "That's everything I know. Stay away from me." He stood up, quickly heading for the exit.

Mason considered following him, but there didn't seem to be any point. He wasn't about to get physical with the guy, and it felt like Leslie had already given up the important part: Qualtrough had been arrested.

Leslie grabbed his coat and hat, glancing back to see whether he was being pursued. Mason watched him leave, taking the stairs two at a time, a streak of camel brown.

Mamie came over, poker-faced, and slid onto the barstool that Leslie had vacated.

"It's amusing to me how so many hardboiled bad guys are just little boys inside," she said, sighing like a world-weary diva in an old film.

"I don't know if I'd call him a boy. He's just a craven little weasel."

"Well, detective, whatever you said worked on him. He looked terrified."

Her jaded expression had been an affectation, he realized, because she was grinning now, happy to be involved in the excitement. She leaned closer. "If the comparison wasn't so insulting to the feline species, I'd call him a pussy."

"He may be that, but he's no fool. Somehow Qualtrough got arrested, and Leslie was there, but he got away."

"Arrested for what?"

"He didn't go into detail, but he said it was lewd conduct. I'm not sure what that means."

"Being friendly with Dorothy is all it means. Anyone in this place could face a similar charge just for being here. If Leslie was with your friend, he's the one who did this—it's a setup. When did it happen?"

"Thursday. Toward evening, I think." He took hold of his bottle of Kronenbourg and gulped from it.

"He may have bailed out by now," she said, shifting to a businesslike tone. "Unless it's a felony vice charge. In that case, he'll still be in."

He looked at her appreciatively. "How do you know all that?"

"Do you not know how much trouble we have with the law?" she said, incredulous. "Dressed like this, I might as well wear a sandwich board that says 'Arrest me: I'm a degenerate.' I can't believe that doesn't happen in Vermont."

"The degenerates are the ones who would arrest you for being yourself," Mason said. "And besides, like you said, you're smart. I know you're a lot smarter than they are."

She preened a little, but said softly, "You don't know that. Not really."

"Intelligence is hard to measure, but it's easy to detect. I watched you working Leslie just now. You were three steps ahead of us both. Don't kid yourself, toots—you're a smart one."

"A smart cookie," she said, and smiled.

"A real smart cookie." He tipped his bottle toward her. "If he's still inside, where will they be holding him?"

"Probably at the jail in Lincoln Heights. Where did he get popped?"

"Pershing Square."

"It's possible he's at the Hall of Justice, depending on when he was arraigned. Try there first. They'll know where he is. But either way, you won't be able to see him at this hour. You won't even be able to pay his bail. Go tomorrow."

"I have to try," he said. "Maybe I can find out if he's been released or not."

"If Leslie orchestrated it, I'll bet it's a felony rap," she said. "He'll be on ice for a while."

He chugged the rest of his beer and asked, "That building is over by City Hall, right? It's the one with the Italianate columns at the top?"

"I don't know about that," she said, frowning. "It's gray. It's right around the corner, on Temple—you can't miss it. It says 'Hall of Justice' over the door."

"Thank you so much for your help, Mamie," he said, meeting her eye. "I never would have gotten this far without you."

"My pleasure, Red. If it turns out your friend needs an attorney, I can set him up with someone who has experience in the field."

"Good to know."

"I hope this isn't good-bye," she said, sincerely this time, not playing the vamp.

"Not if I can help it," he said, and smiled.

He waved to Gus on his way to the stairs, and remembered to take his hat.

He'd never been in the building where Mamie said the jail was, but he knew it, and sure enough, it loomed on the skyline once he was back on Broadway. The stores were closed now, the crowds gone. HALL OF JUSTICE was indeed carved in the stone over the doorway, as Mamie had said, and when he walked inside he was wowed by the opulence of the beaux arts lobby, the white marble, the coffered ceiling. He'd have to remember to try to get in here when he got home—although it would likely be protected by truck bomb–proof barriers and metal detectors, like all public buildings, even though it wasn't a jail anymore. He found a lone sheriff's deputy perched behind a high desk.

"Help you?" the cop asked, looking down at him as he approached.

"I'm wondering if this guy is still in jail," Mason said, holding out the photo.

"What's his name?" the cop asked, not even glancing at the image.

"Qualtrough. With a Q."

"Relationship?"

"He's my brother-in-law."

The cop rose and wordlessly went through a doorway behind his desk, reemerging a few seconds later with a thick black-bound ledger. He sat and flipped through it, seeking the relevant sheet.

"Yeah, he's here," he said, and looked up.

"In this building or in Lincoln Heights?"

"I said he was here. He won't get moved until Monday."

"Can I see him?"

"Tomorrow. No visitors until eleven a.m."

"Can I pay his bail?"

"Eleven a.m.," the cop repeated emphatically.

"Can you tell me how much it is, at least?"

The cop consulted the ledger again. "He's a no-bail."

"Why?" Mason demanded.

"Felony arrest, no papers, and we couldn't establish his identity with Vermont. I guess the judge decided he was likely to flee the jurisdiction."

"Are you kidding me?" Mason said.

It was a rhetorical question spoken in frustration, but the cop answered anyway. "No, I'm not," he said flatly.

"Listen, I can vouch for him—ID him for you."

He shook his head. "That's all in the court's hands now." He closed the ledger and set it aside, then went back to whatever he was reading.

"So is this where I come in the morning?" Mason asked.

"It's where you start," the cop said, a smirk playing on his lips. "Bring a book."

Mason walked back out to the street. He'd found Qualtrough, but he was powerless to get him home. On a felony charge, he could be locked up for years. But at least he'd found him, he reminded himself.

That was huge progress.

He considered going back to the Blue Moon, to ask Mamie about her lawyer friend, but he was exhausted, and his eyes still burned from the smoke in there. He needed to sleep, digest everything he'd learned, come up with a plan tomorrow when his head was clear. Qualtrough wasn't going anywhere.

It took him a long time to find the rooming house again, as the mental map he had of the neighborhood was wrong. The streets were in different places, and there were more of them, some with names he'd never heard before. He finally found it after descending the hill again and retracing his steps from when he'd left it earlier.

He entered as quietly as he could. The house was still, and thankfully the manager's door was closed, no light visible beneath it. He closed his own door gently behind him and snapped on the light. The narrow little bed looked inviting, the thought of sleep overcoming his revulsion at the crummy space. He hung his suit jacket and pants on the hangers in the closet, although he suspected they wouldn't wrinkle even if he dumped them in a heap. Any normal suit would have been a disheveled mess after a day hanging on Mason's shoulders, but this one was pristine. Whatever Kitten had built it with, it was durable. Even the shirt still looked freshly pressed when he took it off.

Pulling back the sheets, he was pleasantly surprised to find that they were clean. He switched off the ceiling light before climbing in, recalling the software at the institute that had done it for him. What a pleasure that had been. The bed was several inches too short for him to stretch out, but if he bent his knees he could get comfortable on his side, his feet resting on the iron bars of the footboard.

He drifted into sleep quickly. Not too long after, he awoke to a familiar high-pitched whine. A point of light the size of a marble winked on in midair, then quickly expanded, filling the room. He sat up in the little bed, baffled, and then figured out what was going on. He got to his feet and stumbled around the sphere, trying to see into it. Then he realized he was naked. Rather than take the time to find his boxers, he pulled his hat off the door and held it in front of his crotch. Stepping farther around the perimeter, he could finally see into the lab at the institute, so brilliantly white and sterile, familiar yet so far away. Annette and Blanchard stood at the control console, peering toward him.

"Do you know who I am?" he called to them, not sure if this connection predated his own arrival at the institute.

"Of course we do," Annette said. "We're in sequence. You left here yesterday."

"OK," Mason said, relieved. Things were working the way they were supposed to.

"Mason, why are you naked, and why are you wearing your hat on your genitals?" Annette asked.

"I'm not wearing it," he said, annoyed. "I'm naked because I was sleeping. I didn't want to flash you my junk."

"How long have you been there?" Blanchard asked.

"Eight or nine hours, I think."

"Is there any sign of him?" he asked.

"I haven't spoken to him yet, but I've located him." He wasn't about to tell them Qualtrough was in jail. It was too disheartening.

"Is he all right?" Blanchard asked. "Where is he?"

"Dude—too many questions. I plan to meet him tomorrow. I'll know more then."

"I'm glad you're making progress," Annette said.

"You go, woman," Blanchard said, clearly pleased.

"I think you mean 'girl.' 'You go, girl.'"

Blanchard shook his head. "I've been researching bygone gay culture, and I'm pretty sure it's 'woman.' You're no girl."

"I'm not a woman either."

"So things are proceeding normally?" Annette asked.

"Yeah, and you can leave a little more time on this end before you reconnect. Give me twenty-four hours or so."

"Understood," she said. "Do you need anything?"

"I'm fine," he said. It was uncomfortable standing there with the hat. "Thanks for dropping in, but I need to sleep."

"Very well," she said, and waved good-bye.

The sphere quickly shrank to a dot and winked out of existence, leaving him standing in the dark holding a hat on his pelvis. He hung it on the door again and stumbled to the bed, where he crashed into deep sleep.

He dreamed of shoji sliding doors, wooden frames with paper panels, moving back and forth in their tracks, somehow passing through one another in physically impossible ways. He laughed as they bent themselves in curves and arced around him. The patterns coalesced, and seemingly random movement suddenly made sense. That's it, he realized, briefly swimming up into consciousness. He knew how to rescue Qualtrough.

TEN

n the morning he lay awake for a long moment in the gray light from the little window, not sure where he was but not too concerned about it, knowing it would come to him eventually. It did, crashing into his consciousness like a thrown brick: Qualtrough was in jail.

After he washed up in the grubby little bathroom down the hall, he dressed and left, glad not to run across the manager or anyone else in the place. The Grand Central Market was right down the hill. It was comforting knowing it would be there, knowing it would be essentially the same. And it was—sawdust on the floor, lunch counters, fruit and vegetable vendors. Nothing even approaching espresso was on offer, so he made do with flavorless cowboy coffee. He bought a container of raspberries and a couple of apples, and ate them at a table in the main hall, slurping down as much of the coffee as he could stomach.

It was almost eleven, according to the clock in the main hall, so he steeled himself and walked over to the Hall of Justice. The deputy at the high desk told him the jail was upstairs, and he rode the elevator, appreciatively taking in the detail in the grillwork, the dark mahogany. Despite the beauty, it was such a serious place, the belly of the justice system. He closed his eyes for a few seconds to quell his unease, telling himself to be calm.

He was concerned about whether he'd actually be able to see Qualtrough, but the visit was routine to the deputies. There were forms to fill out, with questions mostly about him rather than Qualtrough, and he fished his D.C. driver's license out of his pocket to get his fake street address. The cop asked to see it, along with his handwritten forms, and laboriously copied the details into a ledger. Mason had never thought about how time-consuming paperwork had been before electronics. Ned teased him for keeping paper records of his cases, but writing things down helped him think it through. It was mind-numbing watching someone else do it, however, standing in front of a desk.

The cop finally looked up at him to hand the license back. "Are you planning on staying a while?"

"Until I get to see this guy."

"Then why don't you take off your hat?" he said, a command rather than a request.

The waiting area consisted of hard benches in

a windowless, fluorescent-lit room. He'd overheard one of the deputies say it was crowded today, but it didn't seem that way. An afternoon at the DMV in Mason's time made this place look practically abandoned. He sat with his hat in his lap, bored but leery of communicating with the others who were waiting. Most of them looked like moms and dads, wives and girlfriends, worry in their eyes. The place was drenched in human misery. He shifted his thoughts to the more pragmatic issue of what he was going to ask Qualtrough.

At long last a deputy came to the door and called a list of eight names. Mason was grateful to hear his own among them. They were led through two sets of barred gates to a similar windowless room, this one with double desks to keep the visitors away from the inmates, separated by a low wooden wall. The inmates were already there, in denim and blue work shirts, seated in their half of the room. He spotted Qualtrough, but had to look carefully to make sure it was really him. His left eye was ringed in an ugly shade of purple—a classic shiner. He looked thinner, sallow, his hair unkempt and slicked back, his eyes darting around nervously. This was a broken man.

Mason sat across from him. "Christ, man, you look like a ghost."

"Who are you?" Qualtrough asked, apprehensive.

"Blanchard sent me."

Qualtrough's face crumpled with emotion, and he sobbed audibly.

"Don't cry," Mason said, leaning toward the barrier

195

between them. "You'll ruin your makeup."

Qualtrough snorted and coughed, almost laughing.

"We don't have much time. Have you been arraigned yet?"

"Just the initial one, to charge me and say I couldn't get bail. There'll be another one in a couple of weeks."

"Tell me what happened to put you in here on a felony charge."

Qualtrough pulled himself together. "I was set up. This guy I met—"

"Leslie," Mason interrupted. "I know about him. What did he do?"

"We were in the square," he said, "just playing grab-ass. Nothing raunchy, no body parts exposed. It happened so fast."

"What happened?"

"I think the cop might have been in on it from the start. One minute I'm kissing Leslie, and the next the cop punches me in the face and I'm in handcuffs. Leslie just vanished. One of them took my cash, either just before, or while it was happening. So I couldn't even bribe my way out of it."

"Were you drinking?"

"Yeah," he said, looking down.

"You were definitely set up. If Leslie got away, the cop was in on it. Leslie's the one who took your money—he's got a rep as a con man. The cop probably got a cut later."

"I can't believe this is happening," Qualtrough

said, his voice cracking, his eyes pleading. "I wasn't looking for trouble. I just thought there'd be a lot of hot repressed guys."

His own naïveté had landed him here, Mason realized, and it was frustrating that the situation was so intractable. The lot of them, Annette and Blanchard and their whole program, knew what the money looked like, and the suits, and the haircuts, but they were wildly misinformed about the culture.

"Let's try and fix this," Mason said. "That's why I'm here."

One of the guards at the side of the room called out, "Two minutes."

Mason reached into his pocket and powered up his phone, keeping his hand there until he felt it buzz, signaling it was coming to life.

"What day did you get here?" Mason asked. "I mean, when did you step through the portal? Tuesday?"

"It was Wednesday, late afternoon," Qualtrough said. "Is there any way you can get me out of here?"

"If I could tell you one thing to stop you on the day you left, what would it be?"

His lip trembled, but he held it together. "I think I'm special, but I'm not," he said tersely. "I think I can spot a con, but I didn't."

Mason looked sidelong at the guards to make sure they weren't watching and stealthily pulled out his phone. He took a photo of Qualtrough and quickly palmed it again, switching it off and slipping it into his pocket.

"What is that?" Qualtrough asked. "What did you just do?"

"I took your photo," Mason said quietly.

"Why would you bring that with you? It's an anachronism. That might be dangerous."

"Don't be giving me advice," Mason said. "You're the one who landed in jail."

Qualtrough looked like he might break down again.

"Time," one of the guards called, and another moved to open the door for the inmates.

"I'm going to get you out of here," Mason said quickly. "I have a plan."

"Really?" Qualtrough asked, getting to his feet as the guard barked at him to move.

Mason smiled at him encouragingly. "Hang in there. It won't be long."

He stood and watched Qualtrough file out with the others, then followed the other visitors back into the hallway and through the barred gates with the surly guards. Then he strode through the lobby, feeling relieved to be escaping this dark place. He had to get back to the rooming house.

A couple of blocks down Broadway, he stopped short. Standing in the doorway of a drugstore was a familiar face—Hanh, the woman who had rescued Peggy's boyfriend, Matt, when he got stuck, and who had convinced Mason to help her do it. At first he wasn't sure it was her. He'd never seen her wear her hair pulled back like that, and she was in a dowdy high-collared black dress.

She smiled sweetly at him. "I love the hat."

"It is you," he said, stunned. "What are you doing here?"

"Taking you to lunch."

He stood for a minute on the sidewalk, looking at her as the pedestrians navigated around him.

"Are you OK?" she asked.

"I'm just a little … I didn't expect to see you."

"It shouldn't be a surprise, though, considering the things we've done, the places we've been." Hanh watched him, waiting for him to regain focus.

"You mentioned lunch," Mason said after a moment. "I could eat."

She smiled. "There's a diner a couple of blocks from here."

As they walked he looked her over. It was definitely Hanh, he thought, striding briskly to keep up with her confident gait, despite the fact that she was quite petite and barely came up to his shoulder. She seemed lighter today, in a better mood than usual.

She led him to a street corner with a neon sign that said LUCKY. When they stepped in he saw that it was a busy little diner with a counter and booths. Mason hung his hat on the coat rack with the others while Hanh found them a booth. They had barely slid in when a waitress appeared, pencil and order pad in hand.

"Coffee, black," Hanh said.

"The same," Mason said. "And can you bring me a menu?"

The waitress nodded briskly and left.

199

"Such a cute outfit," Hanh said, watching her as she walked away.

"If you say so," Mason said, taking another look. She was wearing a pink-and-white uniform, snug on her ample curves, with a little cap in her hair. He looked quizzically at Hanh; she was usually all business.

"We have to stop and smell the roses in these places," she explained.

"Smell the roses, appreciate the waitress's uniform?" he said.

"Exactly."

Two ceramic cups arrived, perched on saucers, and the waitress slid a menu in front of Mason.

Hanh took a sip of her coffee and let out a deep sigh, as if relaxing for the first time after a long day. "So why do people do such crazy things?"

"Like getting thrown in jail?" Mason asked, looking up from the menu.

"No—like building machines to punch holes in the fabric of reality."

He considered the question. "I suppose it's the scientific drive. To answer all the questions."

"In other words, it's human nature," she said. "'What do you think will happen if we poke it with a stick?' That's the whole history of the species."

"So how much do you know about my week?" he asked, putting the menu aside and wrapping his hands around the hot cup. He knew better than to think this might be a chance meeting.

"The broad strokes." She grinned at him. "In any

case, you got our attention."

The waitress stopped by and raised a harried eyebrow. "What'll it be, hon?"

Not much on the menu looked vegan, but hoping for the best, Mason ordered plain oatmeal, a side of beans, and a side of rice.

"Nothing for me," Hanh said.

When she'd gone, Mason asked, "Who's we?"

"You know," she said. "Laura, from out in the desert. Others. Those concerned with issues of continuity."

He leaned forward and spoke intently. "Hanh, are you a garuda?"

She laughed. "Why would you say that?"

"Matt did some research, and it seems to fit. Garudas patrol paranormal activity."

"I don't know if 'patrol' is the right word, but you've already seen what I do."

"I have," he said. She hadn't answered his question, but he didn't pursue it. It was typical of her not to tell him anything he hadn't already figured out on his own.

"So," Hanh said, shifting in her seat, "once again our interests overlap."

"Qualtrough?"

"The bigger picture—the Sarté Institute."

"Have you been there?" Mason asked.

The waitress set down his dishes, and he started in on the oatmeal.

"Now that they've sent you and Qualtrough through their machine, it's only a matter of time before legions of them are prowling around, far from their own time."

"That's actually their plan. They made this suit, the hat," Mason said, gesturing toward the coat rack with his spoon. "They've got a whole program ramping up to do just that."

"Imagine those people here, or in your LA," she said. "They'd wind up like Qualtrough, or worse."

"Utter chaos," he agreed. "They kept implying that I was a gangster, for no obvious reason."

She chuckled and watched him switch to the rice.

"Whoa," he said, spitting the first mouthful into his napkin. "There's butter in this. It's been a while, but I know that taste." He wiped his hands on a fresh napkin and took a gulp of coffee.

The waitress stopped by. "Everything all right?" she asked.

"Can I get another oatmeal?" he asked.

"You want some eggs, Red?"

"No, thanks—just the oatmeal."

"And more coffee," Hanh said.

She flipped open her pad and wrote down the order, eyeing Mason skeptically, then picked up the plate of rice and his empty oatmeal bowl and moved away.

He pulled the beans over in front of him.

"Don't eat those," Hanh said.

"Why not?" Mason asked, fork poised in midair. They looked like plain old pinto beans—boiled to within an inch of oblivion, but still edible.

"Atmospheric atomic bomb testing."

"What's that got to do with beans?"

"Anything that's high in iodine might have absorbed the radioactive versions of the element while it was growing. Iodine 129 gets spewed into the air in large quantities in an atomic explosion, and there are a lot of those happening these days. Unless you brought a Geiger counter, I'd play it safe."

He pushed the little bowl to the edge of the table, as if it might contaminate him through proximity alone, and unconsciously wiped his hands on his napkin.

He looked back to Hanh, meeting her eye. "Am I out of my depth here?" he asked. "Like Qualtrough? Sometimes I fit right in, but other times I feel completely lost. I never would have thought of radioactive beans."

"So you see the problem with the Sarté machine. You live a lot closer to this place than they do. You can navigate without getting arrested, and maybe you know how a rotary telephone works, but there are still gaps in your compatibility."

"It's definitely a lot more work than I expected." He watched as she drained her cup. "What are you going to do about the machine?"

"We're going to shut it down, of course."

The waitress set down another bowl of oatmeal and refilled Hanh's coffee, shooting Mason a perplexed look as she picked up the bowl of beans.

Mason flashed her a smile. To Hanh, he said, "How does that involve me?"

"I saw that you'd become involved, and I decided

to let it play out. You seem to attract this kind of thing."

"Time slips?"

"I want to say"—she sought the word—"entanglements."

"This was an industrial accident," Mason said, digging into his oatmeal. "Technology-based. It wasn't something that I willed to happen."

"Are you kidding me?" she said sharply. "You know better than that by now. Psychically or not, you got mixed up in it. It's like your friend sitting in lockup. He's not there because of bad luck, or some malfunctioning machine. He made decisions that put him there."

"Am I wrong to be here, Hanh? Am I breaking the rules?"

"No—but don't delude yourself that it was an accident. It was your choice."

"OK," he said, chastened.

"On some level, you're relishing this."

"What do you mean that you're letting it play out?"

"What does it mean to you?" she asked.

"My god, woman—you're always so cryptic. You came after me, remember?"

"Just answer the question," she said gently. "What are you doing here? What's your plan?"

"I came to rescue Qualtrough. I'll take him back to Vermont, then go home."

"That's what I mean by things playing out. You finishing that."

"Then you'll shut down the machine after I'm safely home?"

"'Before' and 'after' become kind of meaningless in this context, don't you think? Remember the idea that everything happens at the same time, and our minds organize it in a linear narrative so that we can make sense of it? We'll take action to shut down the machine in a way that won't interfere with your actions here or in Vermont. Like two ferns growing in a forest, both can unfurl completely."

"But you're going to shut one of them down. Can't the two ferns coexist?"

"Not when one starts punching holes in the other, threatening its integrity. We need to separate them."

"It's a lot to wrap my head around," he said, pushing his empty bowl away. "You're not going to mess them up, are you? I spent some time at the institute, and in their little town. I like them."

She chuckled. "No one gets hurt. Laura is going to the institute at the start of it all to sabotage the technology, not the people, in a very specific way. It'll prevent the machine from ever connecting to the past, and they'll abandon the project before it gets started. We'll gently nudge them in a different direction. Maybe they'll discover something truly useful instead."

"So if I just sit here and wait," Mason said, waving an arm at the room, "this whole thing just disappears? Why should I do anything, then, or enact any plan?"

"Is that what really happens, though? Does it all

evaporate because it never happened? Or does it get siphoned into its own stream to play itself out?"

"That would be appalling," Mason said. "So which is it?"

Hanh shrugged. "Who knows?"

"You do—I'm sure of it. But I don't suppose you're going to lay it out for me." Not that he'd necessarily understand it even if she did try to explain. He sighed, and sipped at his coffee. Now that it was tepid it tasted like dishwater. "So what do I do?" he asked. "Give up? Keep going?"

"You said your plan was to try to save Qualtrough. Regardless of what we're going to do, why wouldn't you proceed with that?"

"I guess that makes the most sense." He thought for a minute. He had the nagging sense that he was missing something.

"Have you ever been to Angkor Wat?" Hanh asked.

Mason shook his head.

"Can you picture it in your head?"

"I could look at a picture of it on my phone, but the cell coverage isn't very good here."

"Try."

He closed his eyes and tried to remember what it looked like from books and travel documentaries. "I can sort of see it."

"It's a beautiful place. What they were trying to do there is show in three dimensions how multidimensional reality is constructed."

"Like a map?" he asked.

"More like a model of reality that includes how time works—all the iterations of a single action displayed, all the moments laid out. No one really knows it's that, of course," she said, and sipped her coffee.

A thought struck him—the thing he'd missed. "If you're saying I should just do what I was planning, why are you here? Is there any reason I need a heads-up about what you and Laura are up to?"

"Well," she said, looking away, "partly it was a courtesy call."

"What else?" he demanded.

"I know that you're planning to use a psychic slip to save Qualtrough."

"OK," he said. He knew her too well to ask how she knew. She wouldn't tell him anyway.

"It's a great idea," she said.

"Is there a problem with it?"

"If you do it, there's a small possibility that you might lose parts of your own reality."

"Seriously?" he asked, watching her closely. "That never came up before."

"It's different because you're so far from your own there-now."

"Would parts of my life be deleted?"

"Not deleted, just shifted around. Like when you toss a wok with a bunch of different vegetables in it," she said. "The pieces move around in new configurations. Things get hidden, other things appear. Shake it a little, and it changes a little. Shake it a lot, and you're a whole new person."

"Will I know that it's happened?"

"Yes, because you left your there-now, and you'll go back to it, so you'll see exactly what changed. It can be disorienting."

"That's upsetting. I don't want my life to change without being part of it." He paused, thinking about it, then sighed. "This psychic stuff—the more I get into it, the weirder it gets."

The waitress stopped by with the coffee pot and refilled Hanh's cup.

"So if I go back to the Sarté Institute tonight without doing my psychic thing," Mason asked, "there's no chance of shaking things up?"

"Correct."

"And what are the chances that things will change if I do it?"

She thought for a moment. "Seven percent."

"Then the decision is easy," he said, rapping his knuckles on the tabletop.

"What are you going to do?"

"I'm going to rescue Qualtrough. I can't leave him here. He's like a fish out of water. I have to help him."

Hanh grinned but didn't say anything.

"You seem so cavalier about the whole situation," he said.

"I see a lot of this kind of thing. I have to maintain some degree of objectivity."

"I get the feeling, though, that you want me to try. Even though it all might evaporate and not even matter."

"It does matter," she said. "We're all responsible for enacting reality."

He nodded. "Right now I can't see it any other way."

She glanced at her wrist. "I should probably get going."

"You know you're not wearing a watch, right? You're checking the time on your bare arm."

"Do you have any money?" she asked, ignoring his question and waving to the waitress for the check.

"Sure," he said, and pulled a few bills from his pocket. She must have forgotten that she had offered to treat him. Not that it mattered—it wasn't even his money.

Hanh took the bills and examined them, running them between her fingers.

"These are good," she said. "They look real."

"Let's not broadcast that," he said quietly.

The waitress dropped the check on the table. Mason left her a dollar, remembered to put on his hat, then paid at the register, following Hanh out to the street. She'd already known what his plan was, and it seemed like an awful lot of trouble to come here just to apprise him of the risk involved. He felt grateful to her for looking out for him.

"I want to give you a hug," Mason said when they were out on the sidewalk. "I know we don't usually do that."

"We do now," she said, and opened her arms.

He gave her a brief, gentle squeeze and stepped back.

"I'll see you soon," she said, and headed down the block.

Lost in thought, he watched her walk away. Just before she turned the corner, something about her shifted. The back of the black dress expanded somehow, and he blinked, thinking his vision was distorted. But it wasn't—he was seeing the graceful curve of wings at her back, black like her outfit, the tips lined with red.

Had he really just seen that? He stepped over to a light pole and braced himself against it, feeling unbalanced. It had been the briefest glimpse, the subtlest hint. He could easily dismiss it as his imagination, or a trick of the light. But he knew what he'd seen. Had she revealed it inadvertently? He stared at the corner where she'd disappeared, behind the gray stone wall of a bank. No, he decided, it had been intentional, a subtle way of answering his question. She was giving him a glimpse of the truth—she really was a garuda.

The idea was disconcerting. Was she a person, or a supernatural entity, or both? In the scant reading he'd done, garudas had wings, but they also had beaks and talons. He couldn't imagine her like that. She'd always been a bit odd, and uncommunicative, even stern, but not inhuman. Today was probably the first time he'd seen her smile, to the point that he'd felt an emotional connection. He had just had his arms around her, and she'd felt real. He couldn't wait to talk to Matt about it. He was going to love this.

Back at the rooming house he went to Qualtrough's room, treading stealthily in the hallway to avoid alerting the manager. He hung his hat on the door and turned on the ceiling light, then adjusted the threadbare curtains to keep out as much of the afternoon daylight as possible. Moving to the closet, he stood inside and reached up, feeling around for his wad of cash, and detached it from its hiding place, stuffing it into his pocket. If things worked out, he wouldn't be coming back here.

Folding his suit jacket and tucking it under his head, he stretched out on the bed, as well as he could, anyway, knees folded so that his legs would fit. He got up again and grabbed his hat, setting it on his stomach when he got back onto the bed, smiling at the memory of greeting Annette with it covering his crotch.

He was confident he could slip through time, because he'd done it before, but he was a little rattled by the potential for permanent changes to his own life. "Ninety-three percent," he said aloud. That meant things almost certainly wouldn't go awry. He started the process of clearing his mind, discarding and suppressing the thoughts that came up, to get his head in the right place. Wednesday afternoon, he told himself. Four days ago. I'm going to bleed through to Wednesday, in a way that won't shake up my life. Breathing deeply, he focused on the idea, focused on that day. He could feel his body relaxing, his mind slowing.

Lying on his back, he was staring directly at the bare bulb above him. He was looking at it but not really seeing it, focused inward instead. The bulb's steady, constant light started flickering, quickly at first but then slowing, until it was a noticeable cycle, bright and dim, on and off. Was he seeing the cycles of the electricity? It was mesmerizing, the slow, methodical strobe. The rhythm permeating civilization. All the turbines and all the lightbulbs connected to the grid, cycling at exactly same frequency, on and off. Everyone in the country experiencing the same ups and downs at the same moment. It was elegant, he thought dreamily, and beautiful. *Wednesday.*

ELEVEN

leep must have overtaken him, he thought, blinking awake, even though he didn't feel tired. He was in the same position as when he'd stretched out, although the light was off now. He felt for the hat, and reassuringly, it was there.

It was Wednesday. He knew it—he could feel it. He stood up and inspected the room. It was the same, empty and quiet. He looked in the dresser drawers, and Qualtrough's notepad was nowhere to be seen. He smiled to himself. There was the proof.

It was only a matter of time before Qualtrough showed up here. All he had to do was wait. He thought about the angle of entry into the sphere, and where he'd tumbled out of it. If he sat near the door, he'd be out of view, and wouldn't scare anyone. He pulled the room's lone chair over and set it there, against the wall. Hanging his hat and jacket on the door, he got as comfortable as he could on the spindly seat, keeping well away from where the sphere would appear.

It was a completely unfamiliar experience, sitting bolt upright in a dimly lit room with absolutely nothing to look at or listen to. He wished he could read something on his phone—the news, anything—but he was alone with his thoughts. It explained why people had been more productive before technology.

He was starting to get a headache, a side effect of the bleed-through, and there was nothing he could do about it, short of hunting down a drugstore. But he had to stay here. He tried to focus his mind away from the discomfort, pushing it to the margins.

After what seemed like an interminable wait, but was probably just an hour or two, the kernel of light appeared in the air before him, accompanied by its obnoxious shriek. His heart pounding, he reached for his jacket and pulled it on as the sphere blew up to full size, then put on his hat, and stood flat against the wall.

As the noise subsided, Qualtrough stepped into the room, effortlessly and without losing his balance, Mason noticed with some annoyance. More important, his plan had worked—he was here at the right moment to intercept Qualtrough. What a relief.

Qualtrough was looking back into the sphere, not yet having noticed Mason. He could hear Annette and Blanchard in the distance, shouting at him in panic.

"I set it to disconnect in a few seconds," he called to them calmly. "Don't come after me."

The sphere screamed and shrank to nothing, leaving the room dim and quiet again. Even in the low light, Mason could see that Qualtrough was nothing like the broken man he'd seen at the jail—he stood there smiling, satisfied at what he'd done, seemingly unworried. When he looked around the room, he saw Mason, and froze.

"Nice tie," Mason said.

"Who the hell are you?" Qualtrough demanded.

"My name is Mason."

"Did she send you?"

"Annette? In a way." He stepped forward, but Qualtrough didn't react, standing there with a puzzled look on his face. He hadn't yet learned to be fearful, Mason realized, coming from the complacent world of the institute.

"I'm not going back," Qualtrough said, his tone belligerent. "I just got here."

"I'm just here to talk."

"How did you get here before me? All the connection slots leading up to this were full. I made sure of that."

"That's not how I got here. I'm not from the institute—I came from the other connection."

"You're a twenty-first-century man? But you said Annette sent you."

"I've been to the institute, but I don't work there. I'm more of an independent contractor. I had to convince Annette to let me hunt for you."

"That woman is a slave-driver. I've never worked for anyone so unreasonable."

215

"And you fixed that by stepping through the machine?" Mason asked, incredulous. "I'm sure you have other motives."

"What I've done is none of your concern."

Mason slid his hands into his pockets. "You're wrong about that. You and I are entangled, Qualtrough. I had to play the Hunter in the festival because you bailed. I'm standing here because of you."

"So you were at the institute after I left, but you got here before me, and you didn't go through the machine. How is that possible?"

"I have my own methods," Mason said.

"There is no other method," Qualtrough said.

"You underestimate me," Mason said calmly, not an accusation, just a statement of fact. "You underestimate people generally, and all of you at the institute underestimate the past. That's a dangerous mind-set. I visited you in jail four days from now."

Qualtrough hesitated, but he was starting to look concerned. "If that's true ... why would I get locked up?"

"You misjudged this place." Mason took another step closer and looked him in the eye. "You think you're special, but you're not. You think you can spot a con, but you didn't."

Something in the words touched a nerve, and Qualtrough's demeanor changed. "Who told you that?" he asked quietly.

"You did. Tonight you're going to a club, where you'll meet a man."

"That's exactly my plan," he said. "That's why I'm here."

"You're looking for hot repressed guys," Mason said.

"Right." Qualtrough's brow furrowed. "We have spoken before."

"Yes—in jail," Mason said emphatically. "Your hot repressed guy is a con man who robs you blind and gets you jailed on a felony charge."

"So how did you get from there to here? You went back to the institute?"

"I'm not going to explain it to you. You're cut from the same fabric as Annette and Blanchard—I know you won't believe it, and I'm tired of arguing about it. But I will show you this."

He pulled his phone out of his jacket pocket and powered it on.

"What is that?" Qualtrough asked. "It doesn't look twentieth-century. You really shouldn't have that here."

"Oh, do not start with me about the anachronisms," Mason snapped.

Once the phone booted up, he found the photo of Qualtrough that he'd taken in jail, and handed the device to him.

Qualtrough peered at the photo and asked, "What's this?"

But from the dismay in his voice, Mason knew that he understood. "It's you, with your spirit crushed."

Qualtrough stared at the image until the backlight went out, then handed it back. "What happened

217

to my hair?" he wondered aloud, and sank onto the bed. He pulled off his hat, a clone of Mason's, and dropped it on the mattress beside him.

"So it's true," he said finally. "I'm not able to pull this off."

"It's not a personal failing," Mason said. "This place is just too foreign."

"But you're managing," Qualtrough said, looking up at him.

"As I said, I'm kind of from around here, so I know how things work."

"I guess I didn't think it through. I can't believe I'd get myself in such a jam."

"But you know it's true. Seeing the photo, hearing me spout your own words back at you."

Qualtrough sighed and rubbed his eyes. "Do you know that expression about turning a ship around?"

"No."

"A ship is big and heavy, not agile. It takes time and effort to change course."

"What does that have to do with you and me?"

"I'm on this trajectory already," he said, his tone brightening. "I'm here. You tell me I've already blown it, but I can't really feel that."

Mason sighed in frustration and ran his fingers through his hair. He instantly regretted it, as his hand now had a coating of pomade. He rubbed his hands together to disperse it.

"Don't get me wrong," Qualtrough said. "I believe you. I accept that I'd get into serious trouble without guidance."

"Guidance? I'm not here to guide you. I'm here to tell you to avoid it entirely, to go back."

"But I've come all this way. Can't we explore just a little? You can keep me out of trouble."

"Too risky," Mason said, shaking his head. "You might end up in jail even if I'm with you."

"How about this," Qualtrough said. "I won't go back with you unless we explore a little first."

"I'm not your dad," Mason said, "and I'm not Annette. I'm not going to make you do anything. I'm leaving here whether you come with me or not."

"OK," Qualtrough said. "Let's just think this through."

"I have thought it through," Mason insisted. "It's pretty straightforward."

"Well, I haven't. Just give me a minute to process it."

"Man, you're going to wind up in jail."

"But that hasn't happened yet," he said. "And now we know how to avoid it."

Mason walked around the room, trying to stay rational and shake off his frustration, leaving Qualtrough to his thoughts.

After a minute, Qualtrough spoke, less glib this time. "Did you enjoy the festival?" he asked.

"I did."

"It brings out the best in people. They can relax, and connect with their friends, and meet their colleagues' families. I really need that right now—downtime. Just a day, or an evening, where I can do something beyond my crazy life. We could go to a club, or even just walk around. I'll behave however you say I should."

Mason understood that desire. His entire psychic career was a reaction to the last soul-crushing office job he'd had. And the alternative to an excursion was to wait for the next connection from the institute, and that would likely be many hours. As long as Qualtrough stayed close, Mason could keep him safe. He was here himself partly for the adventure of it. It seemed cruel to deny Qualtrough the experience.

He pulled the chair out of the corner and sat on it backward, facing Qualtrough.

"Here are the ground rules. Stay close the whole time. Don't go off alone, even to pee."

Qualtrough's face lit up, and he sat up straighter. "Of course."

"No booze."

He frowned. "That doesn't seem reasonable."

"Work with me, man—I'm trying to help you, remember?"

"OK," Qualtrough said flatly. "No booze."

"You can talk to people, and guys, but don't get too flirty. Keep some distance."

"Easy," he said, and nodded.

"I'm taking a risk just being here, Qualtrough," Mason said emphatically. "My whole life is at risk. If you go off-script even once, I'm going to leave you behind and take care of myself."

"Got it," Qualtrough said. "I'll follow your lead."

Mason went to wash the pomade off his hands, and when he stepped back into the hallway, Qualtrough was already there, waiting for him, ready to leave. The door to their room hung wide open.

"Let's go," Qualtrough said, grinning widely.

"Do you think maybe you should take your hat?"

"I forgot," he said, and dashed back into the room.

"Close the door behind you when you come back," Mason called after him. Was this outing a mistake, he wondered? Was Qualtrough really so unprepared that he expected a computer nanny to operate the doors for him? At least he managed to pull it closed without difficulty, and Mason heard it latch.

Ominously, the manager's door was open, and she was standing in the doorway when they walked past.

"Who are you two, and how did you get in there?" she demanded.

"Your son gave me the key," Mason said, flashing her a smile. "I was showing it to my friend."

Her eyes narrowed, and she looked from one to the other, unsure whether to believe him.

"I've decided I'll take the room," Mason said, pulling a few bills from his pocket. Once she'd seen his money, he knew, things would go more smoothly.

"It's fifteen dollars a week," she said, her eyes on the cash.

He peeled off a ten and a five, and added another five when he handed it to her. "A little extra, as a finder's fee," he explained.

She didn't reply, but quickly palmed the cash. Her face softened now that things were settled.

"Sheets are changed Monday," she said, and closed her door.

"She's like a character in a folk tale," Qualtrough whispered as they walked away. "Why did you tip her so much?"

"It's shut-up money. Your machine makes a lot of noise back there, and five bucks will go a long way in helping her ignore it."

They stepped out the front door and down the steps. Qualtrough stopped on the sidewalk, staring at the houses on the street, the cars, the pedestrians.

"It's so … different."

"Let's play it cool," Mason said. "Pretend like you've been here before."

"Just give me a minute," Qualtrough said, and closed his eyes, breathing deeply.

"Are you OK?"

He held up a finger, and Mason waited, nodding to a woman who walked by, curiously eyeing Qualtrough.

"It's so weird here. The smell, the colors. It's shaken me up," Qualtrough said after he'd opened his eyes again, "but I'll manage. Which way?"

Mason led, and gradually Qualtrough regained focus, became confident in his stride.

"The cars are bigger than I thought they'd be," he said. "They look so heavy. Everyone had their own?"

"Not everyone."

"Can we get something to eat?" Qualtrough asked.

"I know some places," Mason said, and they traipsed down the hill. He thought about Clifton's, but it felt too chaotic. The clock outside a bank said it was already after six, so the central market was out.

The Lucky Diner it would be.

When he pulled open the door, the place was quiet. He found them a booth, and Qualtrough followed his lead in hanging his hat on the rack. The same waitress he'd met with Hanh came over to their table, order pad in hand.

"A cup of tea," Mason said, "and a menu."

"What other kinds of drinks do you have?" Qualtrough asked gravely, as if it were a question of utmost importance. Mason tried not to cringe.

"Coffee, soda pop, water," she said, frowning. "What kind of drink do you want?"

"I'll have to think about it," Qualtrough said. "Give me a few minutes."

"Fine," she said, and looked back at Mason. "Matching suits," she said. "That's very sweet. Are you two brothers?"

"Ah—"

"Maybe in a vaudeville act together? Which one's the straight man?"

"Neither of us," Mason said. "We're just friends. But we have the same tailor."

"Matching ties," she said, smiling appreciatively, and as she walked away, "That's so cute."

"How did you talk me into this?" Mason asked.

"You didn't respond to the threat, so I used the soft sell."

Qualtrough was grinning, but Mason wasn't completely sure it was a joke. The waitress set down Mason's tea and slid menus in front of both of them.

"Do you really not know what you want to drink?"

223

Mason asked him.

"I'll have to think about it."

It would be fine if he took all evening to decide, Mason thought, sipping his tea. It would be safer sitting here than in the Blue Moon.

"Hamburger sandwiches, yum," Qualtrough said, perusing the listings.

"So you're not vegan," Mason said. "A lot of the people at the institute were."

"Of course I'm vegan," Qualtrough said, looking up.

"You know hamburger is made out of animals, right? Here, anyway."

"I probably should have known that," he said, looking concerned. "So what's vegan here?"

"Nothing," Mason said. "Coffee, oatmeal, maybe fruit, if you can convince them not to pour cream on it."

"What about the pies?"

"No way. But the fries probably are."

"You were right," Qualtrough said glumly, pushing the menu to the edge of the table. "I'm not really equipped to function here."

The waitress returned and asked, "What'll it be, boys?"

"A plate of fries," Mason said.

Qualtrough looked at her and asked earnestly, "What are fries?"

"What, now?" she said, confused.

"They're potatoes," Mason said, "cut into strips and deep-fried in oil."

"That sounds good. I'll have the fries too."

"Anything else?" she asked, jotting on her pad.

"How about some oatmeal?" Qualtrough said.

"Order it without the fixings," Mason said.

The waitress nodded, but Qualtrough said it anyway. "Without the fixings, please, miss."

"You bet," she said, eyeing him dubiously and writing it down. "Any progress on a drink?"

"I'll have to get back to you," he said.

Mason sipped his tea to hide a smile.

"I'm enjoying this," Qualtrough said brightly after she'd left.

Mason chuckled. "I can tell."

"It feels like a vacation. Like one of those immersion places, only more real, because it is real, you know?"

"I don't. But I'm glad you're having fun."

"Annette pushes so hard. It's good to be out of there. I live in constant fear of screwing something up because she wants it done *now*."

"How's your home life with Blanchard?" Mason asked. "I like him, although it took me a while."

"We have a lot of fun. He's good to me. But he wanted to get serious."

"I saw the ring he was wearing."

Qualtrough looked away, sadness in his face. "So how long were you there? If you were at the festival, that's weeks from now."

"Not weeks from now," Mason said. "Weeks from when you left."

The waitress arrived, her arms stacked with plates.

225

"Fries, more fries, plain oatmeal," she said, setting them down. "Anything else?"

"Do you have green tea?" Qualtrough asked.

"There's only one kind of tea, honey," she said, putting a hand on her hip. "It's what your friend is drinking."

"Oh," he said, leaning over the table to look into Mason's cup. "I guess I'll try one of those."

She sighed and stepped away.

"I was there for a couple of days," Mason said, sprinkling his fries with salt and starting into them. "You'd been missing for two weeks, and they were pretty freaked out about it."

"He's sad?"

"Blanchard? He was an emotional wreck." It was an exaggeration, but he wanted to motivate Qualtrough to go home in any way he could.

"Is he? I kind of miss him, I guess," Qualtrough said, absently munching on a fry. "Whoa," he said, grimacing. "This tastes like machine oil."

"Welcome to the 1950s."

After they'd eaten, Mason paid and tipped the waitress well to compensate for Qualtrough's obtuse behavior. They strolled toward Pershing Square, Qualtrough relishing in the city, though less wide-eyed now.

"My stomach kind of hurts," he said.

"That's because you just ate four pounds of grease. You're not used to it," Mason said, grinning to himself. He felt like he was babysitting a nine-year-old.

"So can we go where the guys are?" Qualtrough asked. "That was kind of the point of coming here."

"There's a place nearby called the Blue Moon. We'll go there. You have to be wary, though. There's a blond guy named Leslie. He was your downfall."

"I'll behave," Qualtrough said cheerfully.

Mason eyed him as they walked. He hoped that was true.

As they walked into the alley and Mason aimed for the familiar door with the faded ½ above it, Qualtrough hung back.

"Are you sure there's a club here?" he asked. "It's so grimy."

"I'm sure. It's in a place like this for safety. They have to avoid drawing attention." He pulled open the door and, before starting down the stairs, said to Qualtrough, "Stay close."

Qualtrough coughed as they descended. "Something's burning."

"Tobacco," Mason said grimly.

The place wasn't busy this early in the evening, just a few guys at tables and a couple at the bar. He spotted Mamie at the far end, perched in the same spot. It was an optimal seat for reconnaissance, he realized. He grinned and nodded to her in greeting. Her eyebrows shot up.

Gus was behind the bar, and Mason hung his hat by the stairs and strode over to him, Qualtrough close by his side.

"My friend Dorothy told me this is a membership-based club," Mason said, before Gus could speak. He pulled a few bills out of his pocket and set two tens and a five on the bar. "This is for two memberships, and when you get a moment, a Kronenbourg for me and a tonic water for my friend here."

"OK," Gus said, thrown off guard. He looked them over, calculating, but didn't move, clearly suspicious.

"Look," Qualtrough said excitedly, pointing to the shelves behind the bar. "They have bourbon. I love that stuff."

"Tonic water for him," Mason said.

Gus looked from one of them to the other. "No monkey business, or I'll throw you out."

Mason held up his palms in mock surrender, grinning at him amicably. Finally Gus took the tens and went through the archway into the back.

The barroom was silent, the few denizens focused on the unknown newcomers. Mason climbed onto a barstool and tried to ignore the attention.

"You get to drink, but I don't?" Qualtrough said, sitting on the next stool.

"That's right. Drinking makes you sloppy."

"What do you know about my drinking?" he demanded.

"Not you specifically. Everyone makes poor decisions when they're blotto."

Gus returned with two blank membership cards and their drinks. He took the five and went over to the register.

"So, does anyone look hot and repressed?" Mason asked.

"All of them," Qualtrough said simply. He swiveled around, surveying the room. "They certainly are interested in us."

"They don't know whether we've come here to cause trouble or not," Mason said quietly.

"Or maybe it's because we're both so good-looking."

Mason chuckled, but he saw that Qualtrough wasn't kidding.

Gus set his change on the bar top.

"Thanks, Gus," Mason said, and tipped his bottle toward him.

"How do you know my name?" he asked, folding his arms. "You've never been in here before."

"That's true, we've never met," Mason said, thinking quickly. "A friend of mine comes here sometimes. He recommended the place, and he told me about you."

"What's your friend's name?"

"Smith," Mason said. "Dark hair, average build. About this tall." He waved his hand vaguely at shoulder height.

"I can't place him," Gus said, still skeptical.

"I'll point him out when he comes in. I'm Mason, by the way," he said. "I'll write it down."

He grabbed the pen and set to work on the membership cards, focusing intently on the task to derail the dialogue. He wrote his own name on one and "J. T. Qualtrough" on the other. He didn't know if Qualtrough actually had any other names, but he wasn't about to ask him now.

Beyond where Qualtrough was sitting, two stools down, sat a guy who was nursing a beer and watching the newcomers as much as he could without gawking. He was dressed more casually than they were, in a cardigan and wool pants, and his hair was clipped in a flat crew cut.

Qualtrough leaned toward him. "Do you like fries?" he asked.

The guy looked surprised. "French fries?"

"American ones, I think," Qualtrough said. "I just had a whole plate of them. Hot and salty and golden."

"I have to admit, I do love a good fry," the guy said, smiling now.

Mason grinned as he forged Qualtrough's signature, then slid the cards across the bar along with the pen. Gus came over to retrieve them.

"Your friend's already gotten into the sauce, it seems," Gus said.

"He's stone sober. He's just a really upbeat person. He lives in a small town, so he never gets to flirt with guys."

Gus cracked a smile. "Well, he won't have any trouble with that one."

Qualtrough turned back to Mason after a few minutes of chatting with the flattop. "You know, it doesn't seem as dangerous here as you said."

"You're not seeing the whole picture," Mason said quietly. "You got arrested for kissing another man in a public place."

"That's illegal?"

"Yes," Mason said emphatically. "This place only

seems safe because it's hidden. That's what the membership is about—you really have to want to be here. And look around you—why is everybody white? This society is completely segregated. I know that's not the way things are where you're from, but Blanchard couldn't even walk into this place because of the color of his skin."

"You think?" Qualtrough said, looking around. "I'm paler than Blanchard, but some of these guys might be almost as dark as him."

Mason looked at him for a minute, amazed. "You can't even see race, can you," he said. "I love that. But it means you can't understand the past. Everyone at the institute thought I was a gangster."

"To be fair, that was the defining characteristic of your time."

"No, it isn't," Mason said, louder than he'd intended.

Flattop leaned toward Qualtrough and asked, "Where were you guys drinking?"

"I'm not allowed to drink," Qualtrough said, jabbing his thumb toward Mason.

Flattop frowned sympathetically. "That doesn't seem fair."

Mason sighed and tuned them out. Mamie was still eyeing them, so he waved her over. She left her drink on the bar and strolled over, her gait languorous and unconcerned, but her eyes betrayed curiosity.

"Hello," she said, playing the vamp.

"Mamie, this is my friend Qualtrough," Mason said.

He had to tap Qualtrough on the shoulder to pull him away from the flattop. Qualtrough glanced at Mamie and said, "How do?" then turned back to his new friend.

"Forgive him," Mason said to Mamie. "He's from out of town." He called to Gus, standing farther down the bar, "Barkeep—a gin and tonic for the lady."

Mamie stood there, pocketbook poised delicately in her upturned hand, looking thoroughly confused. The vamp was gone. "Do I know you?"

"We met a while back, over at The Anvil," Mason said. "You don't remember me?"

"I think I'd remember you," she said.

"You got lipstick all over my mug. Crimson Carnage, you said it was."

"That does sound like me." She frowned. "Was I drinking?"

"I guess. You told me about being in military intelligence during the war, that that's where you learned to wear a dress."

She physically recoiled. "You're scaring me. I have no memory of you."

Mason shrugged. "The Anvil is a rowdy place."

Gus delivered her drink and plucked a dollar from Mason's pile of change. Mamie took the glass and sat on the barstool at Mason's other side.

"I wish I could remember that kiss," she said.

"It was just a kiss," Mason said. "It didn't mean anything."

A few more people had drifted in, and the bar was getting noisier. Gus's helper showed up, ducking under the gate and setting to work washing glasses. Mason glanced at the stairs and caught a flash of camel hair, then looked again—it was Leslie, walking in like he owned the place.

"That guy," Mamie said, following Mason's eyes. "He'll be all over you two. You're fresh meat."

"He'll go for the pretty one," Mason said. "That's never me."

"Consider yourself lucky. He's a little peroxide weasel."

"I know all about that guy," Mason said. He turned to Qualtrough and pulled him away from his chatter. "That's Leslie," he said, gesturing surreptitiously to the bottom of the stairs, where Leslie was hanging up his coat. "He's going to hit on you."

"He's beautiful," Qualtrough said appreciatively.

"No, he's not," Mason hissed. "He's a con man."

"OK, I get it. Don't go home with him."

"Not unless you want to wind up in jail."

Mason wondered if naïveté induced some kind of pheromone, because within seconds Leslie was standing between Qualtrough and the flattop.

"My goodness," Leslie said, laying on his Dixie shtick. "I haven't seen such a fine specimen in ages."

It worked, and Qualtrough was quickly enthralled, focused only on Leslie. Flattop saw that he was being eclipsed and moved away, a resigned look on his face, in search of better prospects.

"Were you in the service?" Mamie asked Mason, and he turned back to her. She was pulling a cigarette out of her handbag, and Mason deftly pulled out his lighter and helped her get it burning. He had a halfhearted conversation with her while also trying to listen to Leslie and Qualtrough flirting behind him. Qualtrough was laughing at Leslie's jokes like a giddy teenager.

Mason turned and tapped Qualtrough on the shoulder. "Are you OK?" he asked him under his breath.

"I'm fine," Qualtrough said, grinning.

Mason could smell bourbon on his breath. "What did we agree on about booze?" he demanded.

"Relax, Dad. I just had a little sip of Leslie's. I'm not getting loaded."

"Don't. I'm worried that you're falling for his mack."

"I am—completely. I'm a sucker for this stuff. But I'm also not an idiot. Just give me a few minutes, and I'll get rid of him."

"Yeah?" Mason said, not convinced, but relieved that Qualtrough wasn't already lost. It would be so frustrating to watch Leslie railroad him, the same pattern playing out again, without being able to stop it.

"Chill," Qualtrough said reassuringly, then turned back to Leslie.

"You're worried about your friend," Mamie said sympathetically. "Is he your lover?"

"Oh, hell, no. He's not from around here, so he's a bit of a babe in the woods. I feel responsible for him."

"He's definitely with the wrong guy," she said, and leaned back, looking past Mason, watching Leslie and Qualtrough. "Do you want me to get between them?

I usually try not to cross Leslie, because he's pals with some dirty cops. But I could easily clobber him."

"I bet you could," Mason said, and smiled. "Thanks, but as long as Qualtrough stays sober, it should be all right."

One of Mamie's friends sat down beside her, and they started talking. Mason finished his beer and flagged Gus down for another one. He knew what he had to do, and he didn't need Dutch courage to make it happen, but as long as he was sitting here, he was going to drink.

He tuned in to Qualtrough's conversation. Leslie was gradually building up the hard sell.

"Oh, the things I'm going to do to you," Leslie drawled.

"Like what?" Qualtrough asked.

"I'm going to make you scream."

Leslie was sitting sideways on the barstool, his head close to Qualtrough's, and when Mason leaned back to look, he saw that he had his hand inside Qualtrough's jacket, in the small of his back, massaging him in a slow circle.

Gus deposited Mason's fresh bottle, whisking away the empty and the unused beer glass, and took some coins from his change pile. Mason drank and closed his eyes, listening to the cacophony of the bar.

"I can't," he heard Qualtrough say, in a soft tone that implied "I might."

"You know you want to."

"I'm with someone."

"Just tell Howdy Doody over there that you need

some fresh air," Leslie said. "I'll meet you in the alley."

"That's it," Mason muttered. He got up and stood behind them. Leslie furtively slid his hand out of Qualtrough's jacket. Mason loomed aggressively over Leslie, hands on his hips, locking eyes with him. Leslie sank back against the bar.

"Keep your grubby paws off my man!" Mason shouted.

The room fell silent. Leslie slid sideways, away from Qualtrough, slipping off the stool and darting toward the door. He grabbed his overcoat and looked back at Mason, terror in his eyes. Mason stood there, temples throbbing, watching him run up the stairs. He knew his face was bright red, he could feel it.

Mamie broke the silence, in a loud voice chanting, "Pop goes the weasel."

Everyone laughed, and went back to their conversations. Mason sat down again, taking a deep breath to dispel the adrenaline. Mamie cackled and slapped him soundly on the back, seemingly forgetting she was in heels and not army boots.

"So aggressive," Qualtrough said. "And all in my defense. I'm flattered."

"I'm just glad he's gone," Mason said.

"You know that I'm not really your man, though, right?" Qualtrough said earnestly.

"Are you kidding me?" Mason demanded. "I've been reassuring people all day that you're not cognitively impaired, but I'm really starting to wonder."

"I hope you know what you're doing," Gus said, stepping over to them. "He's a slippery one."

"I'm not worried," Mason said. "But thanks for the warning." He turned to Mamie. "It was lovely to see you again. I think I've caused enough commotion here for one night."

She smiled. "I'm sure I'll see you around."

"I'd like that." Mason rose and asked Qualtrough, "Ready?"

They walked to the stairs to recover their hats.

"Your change," Gus called after them, waving the bills.

"Put it in the legal defense fund," Mason said, and waved as they went up the stairs.

"Leslie's not going to come back with a firearm or something, is he?" Qualtrough said, nervously scanning the alley as they emerged.

"He's a wrong guy, but he's not that guy. He'll be looking to avoid us."

"How do you know that?"

"I know what motivates him. Getting verbally spanked is embarrassing, but a follow-up would be bad for business. He'll be much more interested in fleecing the next patsy." They rounded the corner onto the street. "So was that enough of a taste of the twentieth century for you?"

"Plenty. Let's walk around a little, though, so I can air out my clothes. Man, the smoke in that place."

They walked over to Broadway, strolling leisurely, looking in shop windows. The evening air was refreshing, and Mason could feel the intensity of the encounter with Leslie melting away.

"You say that these people are dangerous and

segregated and all that," Qualtrough said, "but the only real violence I've seen here was from you."

"What did I do?" Mason asked.

"You went all bully on that guy. 'Keep your paws off my man,'" Qualtrough said gruffly, mimicking him and waving his hands in the air.

"I am not a bully," Mason said, incredulous, stopping on the sidewalk.

"Is that why Leslie ran out of there like the Fox in the festival? I'm not complaining, but I could have handled him myself."

"If I hadn't done that, you'd be eating baloney sandwiches in jail right now."

"Maybe," Qualtrough said. "There's something to be said for managing your emotions and handling things calmly."

"Is that what kept you out of jail?" Mason demanded. "No."

"See? You're doing it right now. It's your first reaction."

Qualtrough stepped to the curb to watch a streetcar roll by.

Mason folded his arms and watched him. Qualtrough's spin on it was infuriating—he hadn't been handling it, he'd been submitting to it. He couldn't see the difference between being calm and being a dupe.

"Magnificent," Qualtrough said when the lumbering vehicle had gone.

"So what did you and Blanchard fight about?" Mason asked, glad for the chance to redirect the conversation. "He said you had a blowout before you left."

"Having kids."

"That's a big one. You wanted them, or he did?"

"Him. I'm not ready. I think I'm too selfish to invest that much time in another person."

"I'm sure you'll be able to work it out."

Qualtrough chuckled.

"What's funny?"

"You want me to believe that so that I'll go without a fuss."

"I guess that's partly true," Mason admitted. "But I also know Blanchard cares for you."

"I know," Qualtrough said. "And I think I'm ready to go back."

That, Mason thought, was very good news.

Back at the rooming house, Mason washed up and then settled into the chair, leaving the bed for Qualtrough.

"It shouldn't be more than eight hours," Qualtrough said, sitting on the bed and untying his shoes. "We've had trouble pinning down the connection times."

"Great," Mason said, shifting in the chair to get comfortable.

"If they're doing things according to our protocols, we'll arrive there a few days after I left."

"They won't know who I am, then," Mason said. "I didn't get there until a few days before the festival."

"How did you explain all that to me again?" Qualtrough asked.

"I didn't," Mason said.

"It seems confusing."

"Yeah, well, I didn't build that damn machine," Mason said. "That's the root of all this confusion. You have to convince them to send me back through the other connection. It took me a couple of days to straighten that out when I was there before, with cops and interviews and all that. But you're in management—you could expedite it."

"I'll try," Qualtrough said, reclining on the mattress and folding his hands behind his head. "I guess I owe you one."

"You know you do. If you need a reminder, I'll show you your prison portrait again."

He left the room light on, but Qualtrough was soon asleep, his hat over his face, his chest rising and falling rhythmically. Mason closed his eyes and tried to clear his mind, to disperse the stress of the evening, and soon he was sleeping too.

Sometime later, he had no idea how long, the room filled with the high-pitched scream of the burgeoning sphere. Qualtrough was already on his feet, his necktie loose, shirttails out. Mason jumped up and grabbed his hat, hustling over to the open side of the sphere. Qualtrough was going to leave half his clothes behind, he thought, standing there in sock feet, but there was nothing he could do about it now. The lab at the institute became visible, with Annette and Blanchard in their white coats.

"He's there," Annette said, relieved.

"Move it," Mason said, "and watch your feet."

Qualtrough hopped through, and Mason dove in after him, this time managing to keep his balance when he landed.

TWELVE

he sphere shrieked and shrank to nothingness. Annette and Blanchard stood there for a second, unmoving, shocked that there was an intruder, or perhaps stunned to see Qualtrough back and half dressed.

Qualtrough ran to Blanchard and fell into his arms.

"You brought someone back?" Annette demanded. "You can't do that. Security!" she shouted at the air.

"He didn't bring me," Mason said, stepping toward the console. "I brought him. I already know you, Annette. You sent me after him."

She looked at him oddly, as if she couldn't parse his words.

"It's true," Qualtrough said. "He saved me."

Louie strode through the door, accompanied by

another cop with the same blue uniform. He glanced at Qualtrough but then focused on Mason.

"Louie Louie," Mason called to him. "Great to see you."

Louie's eyes narrowed. "Do I know you?"

"You will," Mason said. "So are you going to frisk me, or what?" He raised his arms and spread his feet apart.

Louie hesitated, observing him for a moment, and then stepped over and set to work.

"When?" Annette called to Mason.

"When what?" Mason asked.

"When did I send you?"

"The day after the festival."

She didn't look convinced. As he stood there with his hands over his head, Louie methodically went through his pockets, pulling out the contents, then putting things back. He gave his phone a cursory glance but spent more time with Qualtrough's black-and-white head shot, the D.C. driver's license, and the lighter.

"You had me play the Hunter because Qualtrough was gone," Mason said to Annette. Louie had moved down to feel his pant legs; Mason mimed shooting an arrow.

"That's not for weeks," Blanchard said. He'd uncoupled from Qualtrough and was standing behind the console, arms folded.

"I was an amazing Hunter. I missed the Fox by less than three hair widths."

"Qualtrough could have told you all that,"

Blanchard said.

"You think *I'm* lying?" Qualtrough said. "I didn't have to come back here, you know. I came back because of you."

"I'm not calling you a liar," Blanchard said, turning to him. "He could be forcing you to say it."

Louie stepped back, satisfied.

"You build a machine to punch holes through reality, and then you find it hard to believe that I've been here before?" Mason demanded. "What did you expect would happen with all this?" He waved his arms around at the machinery.

Louie looked to Annette. "A couple of things you might want to consider. His suit was made here. So were two of the documents he's carrying, a flame-generating device, and possibly the paper currency."

"Thank you," Mason said emphatically.

"Mason speaks the truth," Qualtrough said. "He talked me into coming back."

"You need to send me home now," Mason said. "Reset the machine and point it to my time."

"If you're from the twentieth century, why didn't you just stay there?" Blanchard demanded.

"Focus, Blanche," Mason said, unable to contain his ire. "I came through the other link."

Blanchard was taken aback. "Don't call me that."

"I knew it," Louie said calmly. "You're not from here. You're way too feisty."

"I'm not a gangster," Mason said firmly. "You guys need to smash that idea once and for all. I want to eat, have a shower, and sleep. That should fill the next eighteen hours. After that, I want to step through your stupid machine and never see this place again."

"I think we need to talk," Annette said finally, eyeing Mason.

"Fine by me, but take me to the cafeteria first. I want that green cauliflower steak, and maybe they'll have the split-pea soup."

"I'll come with you," Blanchard said to Annette. "I'm not convinced this interloper is what he says he is."

"You'll debrief your boyfriend," Annette said, turning to Blanchard. "On the record. Louie, is there anything I need to be aware of?"

"Not at this time," Louie said.

"Mr. Mason," Annette said. "Come with me." She walked toward the door.

"Louie," Mason said, before moving to join her, "tell the system to let me through the doors. I'm not chipped."

"I'll see what I can do," Louie said, watching Mason go.

As he walked by the console, Mason caught Blanchard's eye, and pointed to his own eyes with his fingers, then jabbed a finger at Blanchard: *I'm watching you.*

Blanchard reacted physically, involuntarily taking a step back, completely alarmed. Beside him Qualtrough chuckled and shook his head.

Annette led him through the maze of corridors to the cafeteria. It actually felt good to be here, Mason realized, amid the familiar clean lines and bright lighting. The other cop had followed them out of the lab and was shadowing them along the way. Mason looked back at him at one point, but he wouldn't make eye contact, trailing them stone-faced.

When they entered the cafeteria, Mason saw it was evening, only darkness visible in the broad windows. There were a few people scattered around at the dining tables, and he saw that he raised a few eyebrows, in his vintage suit and hat, but he knew that no one would be too alarmed, considering he was accompanied by the facility's director and supervised by a cop. He grabbed a tray and started loading it up with food from the cases.

Annette watched him forage, and took an apple for herself, joining him at a table after he'd pulled an espresso.

"The food is so much better here," he said to her, setting his hat on a chair and ravenously digging into his broccoli salad.

"Mr. Mason," she began.

"It's just Mason. I'm sorry—I hope I'm not being rude, eating like an animal. I know you don't know me, but I already know you. We did the festival together."

"I believe you," she said, setting her apple on the table. "The suit, and Qualtrough's story, and everything you know about us. There's just one inconsistency." She eyed him closely. "We run the portal in sequence, and I know I wouldn't have changed that to hunt for Qualtrough. It's too fundamental.

So how did you come back here before you arrived there?"

"See what happens when you start messing with this stuff?" Mason said, setting down his fork and reaching for his espresso.

"That's not an answer," she said.

He sipped the coffee and thought about what to say. "I'll tell you truth, and I predict that you won't believe it."

Annette gestured for him to continue.

"I can slip through time using my psychic powers. I can't go far, but I went backward a few days."

She shook her head. "Try again."

"What did I tell you?" he said. "You can believe it or not. It doesn't matter either way." He wasn't about to explain that Hanh was going to prevent this all from ever happening, but he did say, "I'm starting to think that what you're doing here is irresponsible."

"It's not your place to judge us," she said calmly.

"Fine. But I've given you a truthful answer, and that's all I've got." He picked up his bowl of berries and started eating them with his fingers.

Annette took a bite of her apple and watched him thoughtfully for a minute.

"If you are telling the truth," she said, "how did you learn to slip through time?"

"I was out in the desert, and I got mixed up with this extraterrestrial artifact. I think it started then. I'm not the only person who can do it, though—there are lots of us."

"None of whom appear in the literature."

"Maybe you're reading the wrong stuff. Everyone here seems to automatically think I'm a gangster, but I'm not. Neither of the buildings your machine connects to are empty either. You're wrong about that, and lots of other things."

"Tell me what happened when you first got there," she said. "To Los Angeles. How long after Qualtrough did you arrive?"

"Is this a debriefing interview?" Mason asked, glancing toward the ceiling.

"Yes," she said, and smiled encouragingly.

He told her about finding Qualtrough's notes and discovering he was incarcerated. He glossed over going back to Wednesday to intercept him, and described their evening in the city.

"It's an engaging tale," she said.

"It's not a tale, Annette, it's the truth. I have evidence." He pulled his phone out of his pocket and turned it on, waiting for it to boot up.

"We let you take that with you?" she asked, eyeing it askance.

"That's the downside of being so peaceful and passive," he said. "You're not prepared to deal with people from gangster times. I knew you'd say no, so I never brought it up."

She frowned but didn't reply. He pulled up the photo he'd taken of Qualtrough, and handed it to her.

"He's bruised," she said, shocked, staring at it. "All around his eye. I can't believe this happened to him." After a while the screen went dark, and she

249

CHRISTOPHER CHURCH

handed it back to him. "You actually prevented this?"

"You're welcome," he said.

She looked away for a few seconds. She was listening to the computer, he realized.

He waggled the phone. "Do you want a copy of the photo?"

"We obtained a copy," she said.

She went back to listening again, staring into space. Mason waited.

"They're consistent," she said finally. "Your story and Qualtrough's. I guess I should thank you for bringing him back."

"He won't do it again. I think he realizes he wasn't very well prepared for that place."

She looked away again, and then said, "There are some questions."

"Maybe Qualtrough can answer them," Mason said, stretching back in his chair. "I'm falling asleep here, Annette, and I really want to have a shower. I've had Kitten's oil in my hair for days. We can talk again before you send me home."

"All right," she said, and nodded.

"That is the plan, I hope, to send me home?"

"The machine will have to be primed, but yes, we'll do that as soon as possible."

"Thank you," he said, relieved. Looking to the ceiling, he asked loudly, "Where can I sleep for the next twelve hours?"

"One moment," said the familiar voice, right next to his ears.

"By all means," Annette said, gazing into space, "find him a room."

Mason rose and picked up his hat. "Send for me when you need me," he said, and walked toward the corridor at the back of the hall.

"So where are we going?" he asked, and the system guided him, upstairs and to a room similar to the one he'd stayed in before.

When he was stripping down to get in the shower, he said, "Listen—don't take my clothes. I don't care if they're dirty. I want to keep them."

"Understood," the voice told him, and as promised, they was there when he climbed out and dried off, warm and sleepy and happy to be free of the pomade.

He had no idea what time it was, and he didn't ask, because it didn't matter. He draped the suit on the chair in his bedroom and climbed between the sheets, stretching out, smiling at the comfort of it, luxuriating in the feeling of being clean and warm.

"May I ask a question before you go to sleep?" the software voice said.

"OK," Mason said, jarred by the interruption.

"Mr. Blanchard would like to know when, precisely, you first stepped through the portal."

He resisted the first response that came to mind, which was "Tell Mr. Blanchard he can eat my shorts," and instead thought about it, the night he and Peggy had driven over to Chinatown. It felt like so long ago, but he remembered the date and time, and rattled it off. It was a good sign that they wanted to know, implying that Blanchard was setting things up to send him home.

"Lights," he said, and rapidly drifted into sleep.

"Good morning, Mason. They're ready for you downstairs."

Blinking awake, he sat up as the lights brightened, gradually remembering where he was. He went across the hall to wash up and then donned the suit and the hat. The suit jacket wasn't even vaguely gamey up close, despite how long he'd been wearing it, and it still looked newly pressed.

He stepped out into the hall and headed toward the cafeteria.

After he'd made his first turn, the software asked, unbidden, "Can I direct you?"

"No. I need to eat first."

"The director's team is waiting."

"I won't be long."

He ate a banana, drank an espresso, and took an apple to eat on the way. Walking back toward the maze, he said, "Where to?"

As he munched on the apple, the system directed him through the facility to the same staging room he'd been in with Kitten and Lil Dove. Blanchard and Qualtrough were both there, clearly waiting for him. When he walked in and greeted them, Blanchard slid off his stool.

"You're still wearing the suit," Qualtrough said. He looked strikingly different now, no longer a traveler but part of this place again, wearing casual clothes under his lab coat.

"It fits me really well," Mason said, setting his apple core on the worktable.

"It's fortunate that your original departure date aligns with the sequence," Blanchard said. "We'll miss a few slots, and lose those opportunities, unfortunately, but your return fits in after our most recent connection."

"I'm glad you don't have to bend your arbitrary rules," Mason said.

Blanchard looked mystified. "I just said this was going to work. We're sending you home. Why are you agitated?"

"I guess I'm just sick of your bullshit," Mason said, waving his arms. "You asked me to go after your boyfriend with tears in your eyes, and I did, but now you're acting so indifferent—finding a slot in the machine's schedule that won't inconvenience you too much. And you," he said to Qualtrough. "You're completely glib. Do you not understand how close you came to getting stranded in the 1950s?"

"I might not have expressed it in a way that resonated with you," Qualtrough said, "but I do understand."

Blanchard looked rattled, but he clearly didn't want an argument. "We'll aim to open the portal six hours after you left."

"Great," Mason said. "Just enough time for my boyfriend to freak out and start a manhunt. Thanks for that."

But the sarcasm was lost on Blanchard. "You're welcome," he said. "I'm going to the lab. The machine is nearly ready."

Qualtrough watched him leave, then looked at Mason gravely. "Do you remember what we talked about in Los Angeles? About the value of reining in our emotions?"

"Of all people," Mason said evenly, "I am not going to take mental health advice from you."

Before he could respond, Kitten came through the door, businesslike in her lab coat and pulled-back hair.

"Kitten," Mason said, trying to shake off his frustration. "Nice to see you again."

She looked worried. "So it's true."

"Call me Mason."

"I wanted to talk to you about the clothes," Kitten said, ignoring the overture.

"You made this, right?" Mason said, pulling open the suit jacket.

Kitten nodded.

"Well, I love it. I've never been able to wear a suit before this one. I'm going to keep it."

"I don't think that's possible." She frowned. "It's an anachronism. It's not safe."

"The style predates my time, so it's no anachronism. Lots of vintage stores in my day would have clothes like this."

She stood for a moment, looking into space, listening.

"Did we give you money?" she asked.

"Indeed," he said, and pulled out the wad of cash,

254

separating the driver's license and other papers from it. She took the license as well, and the lighter, and the photo of Qualtrough.

"What about gold coins?"

He had hoped she wouldn't think of that. He could feel them under his belt, lined up across the small of his back, six copies of the king's profile, golden and constant, warm from his body heat.

"You know," he said, "Annette gave me a job to do, and I did it—I brought your guy back. Rescued him, technically speaking. So I'm thinking, since I was working for you, the coins are my salary."

"That doesn't sound right," Kitten said, her face clouding.

"They're not an anachronism either, with a twentieth-century king on them."

"I think it would be best if you surrendered them," she said, putting her hands on her hips.

He looked to Qualtrough, but got no support from him. He was following the conversation, but his expression was blank.

"Let's see what Annette has to say, shall we?" Mason said.

Kitten raised her eyebrows, but didn't argue. "We're expected in the lab," she said, and led them out the door.

As they trooped over, Mason thought about how different things felt this time. He'd liked these people before, and he really didn't want to leave here upset with them. He remembered once helping a neighbor free a raccoon that had become tangled in the netting the guy had draped over his boysenberry bushes. Even though they had worn gardening gloves, the creature had managed to slash and bite them repeatedly before running off to freedom, to the extent that they had both gone for tetanus shots. Maybe these people were like that raccoon, incapable of gratitude. If he thought of it in those terms, maybe he could let go of his resentment.

Annette turned from the console to greet them when they entered the lab. Kitten stayed at the door, but Mason held it open for her.

"Can Kitten stay to watch?" he asked Annette.

"Why not?" Annette said, and beckoned her in.

"It's pretty cool," Mason said to her, smiling encouragingly.

Kitten stood a few paces behind Blanchard, who was absorbed in the controls at the console.

"I truly appreciate the opportunity, Director," Kitten said quickly.

Annette nodded distractedly and turned to Mason. "Forgive our confusion. We accept what's happened, even though it's counterintuitive."

"But not surprising, right, given what you've created here?" He gestured widely to the machinery.

"I'm not being clear. What I'm trying to say concerns the clothing and the coins. I accept that I employed you, so let's say you've earned them."

"I think that's a wise decision," Mason said. He really wanted to keep them. The question now was whether they were going to disappear when Hanh rearranged things.

"Full conformity," Blanchard announced.

"It's time," Annette said.

"I've enjoyed getting to know you all," Mason said.

He stepped over and gave Qualtrough a little hug. "Stay out of trouble."

Qualtrough just grinned.

"Be nice to him, you big mook," he said to Blanchard, who looked up in surprise.

Mason walked over to the green box that had appeared in the floor and stood within it.

"Step through quickly," Annette called to him, "and step high so your feet don't intersect the edge."

"I've actually done this once or twice," he said, grinning at her over his shoulder.

The portal blew up, shrieking from a speck of light into the familiar rippling sphere. He felt a surge of adrenaline being so close to the noise and light. Soon he could see the mottled wall of room 203. It was the right place—that was a relief. He turned back to the group, said "Ciao," then took a deep breath and stepped over the threshold.

THIRTEEN

ust in case he was going to lose his balance again, he dropped to all fours as he hopped through. The sphere shrieked to nothingness, and he crouched there for a moment, listening, letting his eyes adjust to the dim light. It was quiet, and it was still dark outside the grimy windows. If he'd landed six hours after he'd left, as Blanchard had said, it would be daylight. That made him uneasy, beyond the jarring shift in his environment. How far off was he?

Once he was sure he wasn't going to fall over, he stood up and pulled his phone out of his jacket pocket, switching it on. "Clock set to network time," the screen told him after it booted. He didn't know the exact moment he'd left, but the date was the same, and the time on the screen had to be close.

Could that be right?

He froze when a muffled voice came from the hall.

"Did you hear the noise again?" It sounded like Peggy.

He stepped out into the hallway, and saw that the restroom door was closed. He walked over to it.

"Are you in there?" he asked tentatively.

"Of course I am," she said. "Did you go back in the haunted room?"

A lump came to his throat, and he put his forehead on the door. It was overwhelming, finding her here. Blanchard's timing was so imprecise that the portal must have opened right after he'd left. He shuddered to think what would have happened if the two events had overlapped.

"Mason?" Peggy called. "You'd better be out there."

"I'm here," he said, and grinned.

"So it happened again?"

"Yes."

"It's stopped, hasn't it?"

"Yes," he said, and swallowed hard.

"Don't go back in that room," she called through the door. He heard the toilet flush. "You know, she might also be a junkie."

"What?"

"The tat," she said, louder. "'Only god can judge me.' A junkie would get a tattoo like that."

He laughed. The artist. He'd carried a box of her stuff downstairs. It seemed like years ago.

"It's no joke," Peggy said. "That'll be on her skin for all time. She should have had it done backward, at least, so that she could read it in the mirror."

The door swung open, and Mason stepped back. She came out into the hall and froze.

"Mason?" She looked shocked.

"I love that flannel shirt," he croaked, feeling his eyes brimming.

She stared at him for a second, then pulled him into a hug. "You smell like smoke." Stepping away, she looked him over. "How long were you gone?"

"How did you know?"

"You look thinner. And three minutes ago you weren't dressed like Buster in Ned's old movies. Or on the verge of tears."

He hastily wiped his eyes. "It's hard to say. Maybe a week or ten days."

"The window, into the white room ... you stepped through it."

"I did."

"This is very weird." She pushed her long hair behind one ear.

"I know," he said, grinning like an idiot, staring at her. It was a relief to see her, to see that she was the same, that she hadn't been rearranged out of his life. Peggy, at least, had managed to avoid Hanh's seven percent chance of revisions.

"What do we do?" Peggy asked.

"We leave. I know what's going on here now."

"You don't have to ask me twice," she said, and moved toward the stairs.

Mason followed her out to the dark street, the building's heavy front door slamming behind them.

Her Prius was parked where they'd left it.

"It's the same," he exclaimed.

"Why wouldn't it be?" she asked, climbing into the driver's seat.

"I guess I'm just happy to be back," he said, pulling off his hat and tossing it in the backseat, then climbing in beside her. Nothing felt like it had been rearranged, not yet. He had a sudden thought. "How's Ned?"

She shifted into gear and pulled away from the curb, shooting him an odd look. "Why would you ask that?"

His heart started racing. "Uh …"

"You saw him when I did. I'm sure he's still in bed."

"Right," he said, relieved that her memories paralleled his own, that Ned still existed.

"Mason—what the hell happened in there?"

"Well … basically, some scientists from the future punched a hole into room 203. That's what we saw, and that's what all the noise was."

She drove in silence for a minute. "How far in the future?"

"I'm not sure. A century. Maybe longer."

"And you went there? And they gave you a vintage suit?"

"I'm sure it's hard to believe."

"Extremely hard to believe. But I saw that window too, with the geeky-looking people inside." More gently, she added, "And I can see it in you." She didn't look at him, gazing out over the steering wheel. "You've changed. I can tell you were gone."

"I'm so glad I'm back," he said.

"What were they like?"

"They're all really docile. They thought I was aggressive."

"You?" she said emphatically.

"By comparison, I guess I am. At least they had vegan food."

"What are you going to tell Yoshida?"

"Yoshida. I almost forgot that's why we're here." He knew why she was concerned about that. Even though she believed him, she didn't want other people to see him as untethered from reality. He thought about it, watching the dark city roll by. "He's a pragmatist, so I won't be telling him the truth."

"Good."

"I'll tell him the ghost activity is going away. I'll come up with a reason."

They rode in silence for a while.

"Why does this stuff happen to you?" Peggy asked finally.

"Hanh says I attract it. It's connected to the paranormal work. She says I relish it."

"Do you?"

"I think I do, yeah."

"Well, your life is definitely getting weirder with every passing day."

Peggy always left her car on the street, because the garage was reserved for Ned's babies, his vintage

Barracuda and classic Crown Vic. As they walked up to the house from where she found a parking spot, Mason realized he didn't have his keys—they were in Vermont, caught in an invisible slice of reality that had folded in on itself, lost forever.

Peggy unlocked the door and kicked off her sneakers. She looked exhausted. "Get some sleep," she said quietly, before disappearing into her room.

Mason found some leftovers in the fridge and nibbled for a few minutes before treading softly down to the bedroom. His heart swelled at the sight of Ned, sound asleep. He watched him for a minute, admiring his vague form under the sheets, listening to his rhythmic breathing.

He had no idea how much he would reveal about his trip, but he knew he had to tell him about kissing Mamie. But that was a challenge for another day. He found a pair of sweatpants and a T-shirt, then went back to the kitchen, closing the bedroom door behind him.

Changing out of the suit, he spent a few minutes working the gold coins out of their tight little pouches, lining them up on the countertop to admire them. What was it about gold? Next he emptied the pockets, then got a trash bag and folded the clothes into it, tying the top shut. He'd get the suit dry-cleaned, even though it still looked pristine. That would get rid of the smell of smoke.

Scooping everything up, he went to the office and dropped it on his desk, then pulled open his bottom drawer, finding a blank manila folder and putting all the detritus in it—the membership card for the Blue Moon, Qualtrough's handwritten bar list, the book of matches. On the folder's tab he wrote QUALTROUGH in block letters, then slipped it in with his other case files. A thought struck him, and he spent a minute digging through the folders, looking for possible rearrangements or missing files. All his cases were there, and nothing seemed to have changed. He took a deep breath. That was a relief.

The coins went into his top desk drawer, out of sight under all his pens and pencils. He took the trash bag into the bedroom, quietly setting it in the bottom of his closet. He wasn't tired at all, as he'd had a full night's sleep just a few hours ago, but maybe a long hot shower would make him sleepy.

Ned didn't stir when he climbed into bed, even when he moved close to him, enjoying the contour of his body. He lay there for a long time, running through his head what he was going to tell Yoshida, what he was going to tell Ned. He fell asleep late. In his dreams he came across Mamie, dressed to the nines and playing the coquette. She arched her eyebrows and leaned close. "Only god can judge you, Red."

FOURTEEN

ven though he hadn't slept for very long, he woke early, and heard someone in the kitchen. He pulled on a pair of pants and a sweatshirt and went out to find Ned at the counter eating toast. He turned as Mason came in and did a double-take.

"What happened to your hair?" he demanded.

Mason pulled him off the stool into a long hug, trying not to get tearful.

When he let go, Ned gently took his hands in his and examined his face. "What's going on?"

"It's kind of a long story."

Peggy came in, dressed in sharp conservative gray for work. "Break it up, you two," she said.

"Breakfast?" Mason asked her.

"I ate already, but thanks." She pulled on her

dressy black work shoes.

"What happened to him last night?" Ned demanded. "Who cut his hair?"

"You haven't told him anything?" she asked.

"I just got up," Mason said.

"So we walk into the building," Peggy said, meeting Ned's eye, "and it's really spooky. There's a staircase leading up to the second floor, and we're standing there, and this baby carriage comes tumbling down the stairs." She mimed the action, rolling her hands over each other. "I don't know what happened next, because I ran out."

Ned laughed and said, "Nice try."

"I had you for a minute, though, didn't I?"

"Not even a nanosecond."

"Good luck," she said, eyeing Mason, then waved good-bye and headed out.

Ned looked at his watch. "If it's one of your crazy work stories, can we talk after lunch? I've got to meet some people."

"Suits me," Mason said, happy to have a brief reprieve, not even taking umbrage at the turn of phrase.

Before long Ned was gone too. Mason had breakfast, fruit and bread, then went into the bathroom to look at his hair in the mirror. It wasn't a bad haircut, he thought, adjusting it roughly, but it didn't really suit him.

At his desk he pulled out his phone and called Yoshida, who picked up after a couple of rings.

"I went to your building last night," Mason told

him, "and I have some insights. Can I can drop by later on?"

"Excellent news," Yoshida said. "You work fast. I'll be at Rugley any time after three."

Many of his clients paid him in cash, which had started accumulating on its own at the back of one his desk drawers. He left a small stack there for contingencies, and pulled out a wad of it now, then went to the kitchen, where he scrabbled around in the junk drawer until he found the spare front door key. He'd have to get a full set made, but at least with this he could leave the house. Without his keys he couldn't lock up his bike either, he realized. He had a spare set somewhere, but rather than hunt for them, he decided to walk.

It was just a few minutes' down the hill to the boulevard and Mr. Harry's House of Hair. On the walk he appreciated the feeling of the morning sun on his face, the still, cool air. He looked around at the foliage and the cars, grinning at the familiarity. It was a mundane street, but he hadn't seen it for ages. Most significant, this place felt right—it was definitely home.

He had no idea who Harry was, he realized, as he pulled open the door to the salon. There were a couple of stylists working, and his usual guy, MJ, was free. He claimed to run marathons, despite having a distinctly nonrunner's body, his paunch hanging over his belt, and his hair was long and unkempt for someone working as a barber. But he was in Mason's price range—he could have MJ cut his hair every day for what Ned spent on his hair every few weeks—and he did a good job.

"What happened to you?" MJ asked, looking up from the counter.

"That's exactly what I said when I looked in the mirror this morning. Can you fix it?"

MJ soon had him in a chair, snipping and clipping, telling Mason all about training for an upcoming race in Missouri.

"You should try it," he said. "Our bodies were designed for persistence running. There's nothing like it to keep you in shape."

"OK," Mason said dubiously, feeling the pillowy softness of MJ's belly against his back as he leaned in for the precision work.

Before long MJ was brushing the fallen hair off his shoulders, and Mason was satisfied with the look. He paid him and walked back up the hill.

Before long he heard the garage door, and Ned coming in. He took a deep breath and steeled himself. Miss Cassie was right—he knew he needed to tell Ned the truth about what was going on, about his experiences, and this one was too big to soft-pedal. The hard part was going to be about Mamie. He had been dreading this moment, but now that it was inevitable, he was anxious to get it over with.

When he came out to the living room, he found Ned sprawled in an easy chair, regrouping from his outing. He was dressed for work, sleek and polished, his fitted shirt immaculate and showing off his pecs. Mason sat across from him on the sofa.

"You cut your hair again?" Ned asked, taken aback.

"It looks better, doesn't it?"

"Of course. You look like a hundred bucks."

Mason chuckled. "After what I've been through, I'll take it."

"So what happened last night?"

"Well, you were right that there's a scientific explanation for Yoshida's ghost."

"I knew it," Ned said, thumping the arm of his chair.

"I'll explain it all, but I have to tell you a specific part of it first." Mason sat forward on the sofa, hands on his knees.

"You look worried," Ned said, mystified.

"I am." He took a deep breath. "So at one point I wound up in a bar—"

"With Peggy?"

"Just me. So I'm in the bar, and this guy kissed me. A drag queen."

Anger flashed in Ned's eyes. "Damn it, Mason, how could you do that?"

"I didn't encourage it. We were talking, and it just kind of happened."

He absently clenched and flexed his hands, his chest heaving. "What did you do?"

"I let it happen for a second, then I stopped it. It didn't mean anything."

"Nothing else happened?"

"Of course not."

He sat quietly while Ned thought it through. His initial anger was already fading, Mason could tell. Latin blood, Ned had explained, was quick to boil but quick to cool off too.

"Was he a better kisser than me?" Ned demanded.

"No way. Not even close."

"I won't say I'm not upset, even though I know that's probably irrational." He watched Mason for a minute, calculating.

Mason held his tongue. He knew there was nothing he could say that would make it easier.

"Here's the deal," Ned said finally. "As compensation, you owe me several hours of the sexual activity of my choosing."

Mason laughed, relieved. "That I can do."

"How did you wind up in a bar?"

Mason sat back and got into it, making it sound as rational and logical as he could. He skipped the part about the festival, and about moving backward with psychic power. If the scientists who'd seen direct evidence of it didn't believe it, there was no way Ned would.

Ned asked a couple of questions, clarifying the details, trying to pin down more about the Sarté Institute. When he'd absorbed it all, he folded his hands behind his head. "My god, Mason—craziness is attracted to you like soy sauce to a white shirt."

"So you believe me?"

"Let me digest it first. You look thinner, and I know that couldn't have happened overnight. Peggy saw the portal?"

"Ask her. She was there right before I stepped into it."

He got up and sat with Mason on the sofa, folding his hand into his own. "I'm glad you led with the infidelity part."

He gently rubbed Mason's short new hair, feeling the bristles. Mason could hear him breathing, the emotion in his body.

"Don't kiss other people," Ned said intently.

"Deal," Mason said, and kissed him, lingering, getting lost in it.

Afterward he went back into the office and searched through his desk until he found the spare key to his bike lock. Ned was at his own desk, absorbed in his work.

"I lost my keys," he said. "I found the front door key in the kitchen, but do you have an extra set that I can make copies of?"

Ned swiveled his chair around to face him. "Is there any way someone will find them and figure out where you live? I can change the locks."

"No chance. I left them at the research institute in Vermont."

Ned stared at him for a moment. "You have a very odd life." He dug around in his desk and found the keys, tossing them over to Mason.

He'd stop at a locksmith on the way back from seeing Yoshida, he thought, dropping the keys into his pants and kissing Ned good-bye. He slung his backpack on and walked out to the garage, where his trusty steed stood right where it always was, far enough from Ned's cars that he couldn't be accused of causing them any scuffs or scratches when he parked it. Ned kept the garage immaculate, tools arranged neatly on the wall, nothing ever left on the floor. It struck him as odd, then, that there was a pile of dead leaves on the workbench. They were the distinctive broad leaves of the plane trees that lined part of their street. This was the season when they turned brown and fell, creating a riotous messy carpet for a week or so before they got swept away. He was about to wheel his bike out, but it struck him that Ned would never have brought those in. If they'd blown in or had ever passed through Ned's hands, they would have wound up in the trash bin, not in a neat little pile.

He scooped them up, intending to drop them in the trash, and underneath found a sheaf of folded paper, and under that a set of keys. He stared at them for a moment, disbelieving. They were his, unmistakably—a distinct key for his bike lock, and then the laminated library card. His skin crawled, and he glanced around the quiet garage. He knew what the papers were too, knew what they had to be. Fingers trembling, he unfolded them to make sure. It was the notes he'd written the day of the festival, sitting in the cafeteria at the institute.

He dropped the keys in his pocket, and pulled off his backpack to slide the notes inside. His heart was pounding. It had to be Hanh, he realized. There was no other reasonable explanation. But why under a pile of leaves? He thought of the glimpse of black wings, then glanced around the garage again, at the hulking cars and the neat array of tools, reassuring himself that this was all real. He scooped up the leaves and dumped them in the trash. There was more going on in the world than he'd ever know.

Rugley Hall was an easy bike ride, and Mason took side streets most of the way, thinking about the keys and his notes. There was an element of humor in having them appear like that. They weren't essential to his survival, but he was still glad to have them, especially the notes. It made it more permanent, reaffirmed that it had really happened. Perhaps that was part of the reason they'd come back to him, to remind him of it, to fix the experience in his memory.

He locked up his wheels at Rugley Hall's bicycle rack and nodded to the security guard as he made his way to Yoshida's office, rapping lightly on the wooden door.

"Come in," Yoshida called, and rose to greet him with a smile. "So you visited the Montclair Security Building."

"I did. I met one of your artist tenants too," Mason said, slipping off his backpack and dropping into one of the chairs in front of the desk. "She was moving the last of her stuff out."

"They should all be gone by now," Yoshida said, reclining in his chair. "You said there was news."

"Do you know what infrasound is?"

"I can't say that I do."

"I don't understand it very well either, but from

the research I did, it seems that certain sound frequencies can induce feelings of dread in people. Infrasound is very low frequency, so you can't hear it, but it can have an effect on your mind and spark a fear response. That feeling can be mistaken for something supernatural."

"How did infrasound get into the Montclair Security Building?"

"Old plumbing and heating equipment vibrate, which generates it. There are a lot of old pipes and ducts in that building. I didn't have any equipment to detect infrasound, but I could feel that sense of dread when I was in room 203. When I cut the power and went back in, it was gone."

"Fascinating," Yoshida said, sitting forward. "So the story about the gray woman?"

"That came from a creative mind. You know how artists are."

"I do indeed." He nodded. "The pipes and heating ducts will all be replaced when I renovate."

"For now, though, you could put a door on room 203 and keep it locked. Tell the tenants the ghost is in the ductwork."

"It sounds like you've figured it out," Yoshida said. "Thanks for your hard work."

"My pleasure," Mason said, rising from his chair.

"Before you leave, what do I owe you?"

Mason had forgotten about that—this was a paying gig. The dreamy glimmer of six shiny gold coins had diverted his focus.

"I wasn't in the building for long, and I figured it

out pretty quickly. I did spend some time on research, though," Mason said.

"How about five hundred?" Yoshida said.

"That sounds fair." Considering he would have walked out with nothing, it was probably more than fair.

Yoshida clicked open his briefcase and pulled out a checkbook, scribbling the details while Mason waited. "You'll have to invoice me, for my records," he said. "Just use the word 'research' and include the name of the building."

"I'll do that," Mason said, taking the check and slipping it into his backpack.

"I'm glad there was a simple explanation. That's usually the case, don't you find?"

"Not always. But it's a good rule of thumb."

He said good-bye to Yoshida and went back out to the street, unlocking his bike. He felt lighter with the meeting out of the way. As he rode away, he craned upward to look at the grand building and the trees lining the street. Plane trees, he realized with a smile. The street was carpeted with their brown leaves.